"Drop your guns, real slow," Fargo said. The two men stared at him, and Fargo saw their gazes go to his hand as it rested on the Colt. He saw the thought forming in their eyes at once—his gun wasn't out, he had no advantage over them.

"Easy, mister, whatever you say." The one with the mustache slyly grinned.

Fargo sighed. "Don't do anything dumb," he said almost wearily.

Then he saw their fingers as they touched their guns. Fargo drew the Colt with the speed of lightning, the revolver up and firing while both men were still yanking their guns out. The shots hit home and the two men dropped, hitting the ground at the same time. Fargo stepped toward their silent forms and muttered—

"I said don't do anything dumb."

THE

TRAILSMAN

#215

DUET FOR
SIX-GUNS

by

Jon Sharpe

A SIGNET BOOK

SIGNET
Published by New American Library, a division of
Penguin Putnam Inc., 375 Hudson Street,
New York, New York 10014, U.S.A.
Penguin Books Ltd, 27 Wrights Lane,
London W8 5TZ, England
Penguin Books Australia Ltd,
Ringwood, Victoria, Australia
Penguin Books Canada Ltd, 10 Alcorn Avenue,
Toronto, Ontario, Canada M4V 3B2
Penguin Books (N.Z.) Ltd, 182–190 Wairau Road,
Auckland 10, New Zealand

Penguin Books Ltd, Registered Offices:
Harmondsworth, Middlesex, England

First published by Signet, an imprint of New American Library,
a division of Penguin Putnam Inc.

First Printing, October 1999
10 9 8 7 6 5 4 3 2 1

The first chapter of this book originally appeared in *Texas Hellion*,
the two hundred fourteenth volume in this series.

Ⓟ REGISTERED TRADEMARK—MARCA REGISTRADA

Printed in the United States of America

The Trailsman

Beginnings . . . they bend the tree and they mark the man. Skye Fargo was born when he was eighteen. Terror was his midwife, vengeance his first cry. Killing spawned Skye Fargo, ruthless, cold-blooded murder. Out of the acrid smoke of gunpowder still hanging in the air, he rose, cried out a promise never forgotten.

The Trailsman they began to call him all across the West: searcher, scout, hunter, the man who could see where others only looked, his skills for hire but not his soul, the man who lived each day to the fullest, yet trailed each tomorrow. Skye Fargo, the Trailsman, and the seeker who could take the wildness of a land and the wanting of a woman and make them his own.

*Colorado, 1860, where casinos sprang up to cater
to the grifters and drifters, ranchers and rangers,
cattlemen and cowpokes, bumpkins and bankers.
They offered every kind of amusement but too
often served death and deceit. . . .*

1

The big man on the magnificent Ovaro let a smile of
appreciation touch his lips as he drew in the full, rich
beauty of the land. This was fertile, fecund terrain
where the lower Colorado River nestled between the
San Juan and Sangre de Cristo ranges of the Rocky
Mountains. Towering stands of cottonwoods, blackjack oak, red cedar, and aspen mingled with wide open
rolling fields. Vast banks of fireweed, their vibrant
pink spires shimmering in the sun, edged equally
wide carpets of Rocky Mountain iris, their blue-violet
leaves infused with purple veins. In the distance, a bed
of delicate yellow brittlebush formed a striking con-
trast of shape, texture, and color.

But suddenly the big man's lake blue eyes narrowed
and turned cold as an ice floe. His lips thinned and
anger knotted his stomach. When beauty was marred,
loveliness defaced, anger always stabbed at him. It
could be an ugly stain on a lovely garment, a shattered
hole in a beautiful vase, a delicate painting ruined by
a jagged tear, a fine horse with a badly swollen, ne-
glected hock. It didn't make much difference what. It
was beauty defaced, splendor marred, loveliness destroyed that affronted him, and now it had happened
again, unexpectedly. But it was always unexpected, he

reminded himself. This time it was black-winged, ugly forms slowly circling through the sky that defaced the beauty of the scene. He watched their almost motionless flight and knew them for what they were—symbols of death, messengers of decay.

Skye Fargo moved the Ovaro forward, his eyes following the slow, downward spiral of the huge, black wings just beyond a small shrub-covered rise. Pushing his way through a stand of tall vervain, he crested the rise, his frown deepening as he saw two figures on the ground, both young women, both lying on their backs. A half-dozen buzzards walked across their lifeless bodies. Powerful, hooked beaks at the end of red-skinned heads tore strips of flesh from the two still forms. Fargo drew his Colt when he suddenly saw he was not alone at the grisly scene. *Goddamn*, he cursed silently. Two horsemen emerged from a line of red cedars across from him, both wearing only breechcloths and armbands. He immediately backed the pinto down the rise until he was out of sight behind the vervain. He watched the two horsemen approach the figures of the two young women, swinging from their ponies with smooth, lithe movements. The buzzards reluctantly took wing as the two men stepped to the bodies.

Fargo's eyes fastened on the armband of one of the Indians, seeing the distinctive beadwork design. "Wind River Shoshone," he muttered as the Indian bent down to one of the young women. He curled a hand around long, blond hair and pulled her head up. He drew a hunting knife from the thin, rawhide waistband of his breechcloth and started to bring the knife down to the woman's head. "Look good hanging on teepee pole," the Indian said to his companion. Fargo knew the Shoshonean language well enough to understand. Drawing the Colt, Fargo started to bring it up, but then dropped it back into the holster. The two Shoshone might have friends nearby, he reminded himself. As the Indian pressed the edge of the knife against the young woman's scalp, Fargo spurred the Ovaro forward over the rise.

"No, you don't, you two-handed vulture," Fargo bit out, seeing the Shoshone drop his hold on the girl's hair as he spun. But the pinto was charging at full speed, and as the Shoshone raised the knife to strike, he had to quickly duck away as the horse bolted toward him. Fargo leaned from the saddle, brought the Colt out and down in a sweeping blow that grazed the Shoshone's head. The Indian pitched forward, and sprawled facedown on the ground. He shuddered, then tried to lift himself up but Fargo had already leaped from the saddle, landing only a foot from the Indian. This time, the Colt crashed down on the man's head with full force. The Indian collapsed and lay still. As Fargo whirled, the second Shoshone charged at him, a tomahawk raised in one hand. The Indian brought the short-handled ax down in a furious chopping blow that Fargo easily ducked, then ducked away again as the Indian attempted a flat, sideways blow. Fargo shifted his hold on the Colt, his fingers closing around the barrel to leave the heavy butt free.

Once again, the Indian swiped viciously at him with a short, quick chop of the ax that Fargo barely avoided. The Shoshone, a slender but tightly muscled figure, shot two more blows at him with his war ax as Fargo tried to strike at the man's head with his Colt. He had to drop low to avoid the Indian's catlike reaction, the tomahawk grazing his scalp as the Shoshone struck

3

out. Once again Fargo narrowly avoided the tomahawk's sharp edge, realizing the Shoshone was ex-
tremely fast with his weapon. Circling, Fargo feinted
and saw the Indian move with him, ready to strike a
counterblow at his first chance. Fargo started to move
in, swinging wildly with the Colt. The Indian easily
avoided the blows, striking out with his own coun-
terblows in quicker, more accurate responses. Fargo
saw the Shoshone wait in a half crouch, confident that
it was but a matter of time before his strokes hit their
mark.

He waited for Fargo to come at him again. Fargo
obliged, feinting left, then right, and the Shoshone responded, bringing the tomahawk down in quick, vicious arcs. Fargo made another feint and the Indian
struck back at once. But this time Fargo didn't try to
reach the man's head. Instead, he brought the butt of
the Colt down on the Shoshone's wrist as the man
swung the ax down in another counterblow. He heard
the man gasp out in pain as the butt of the Colt
smashed into his wrist, instantly hitting bone, tendon,
and nerve. The tomahawk dropped from the man's
hand as Fargo brought the Colt around in an upward
arc, smashing it into the Indian's jaw. The Shoshone
staggered backward, his jaw suddenly hanging open
at a grisly angle. Fargo swung the Colt with all his
strength, and the Shoshone's forehead split down the
center with a rush of scarlet.

The brave fell in a heap at his own feet and lay still.
Fargo straightened, drew a deep breath, and turned
the Colt in his hand as he strode to the two young
women on the ground. Kneeling, he examined their
dresses, finding only empty pockets with nothing to
identify either young woman. As his eyes moved

4

across both of their bodies, a furrow dug into his brow. The wrists of both young women bore circular bruise marks. They had plainly been bound. Then, amid the scars from the vultures, he saw the round holes in each of the young women's breasts. It wasn't hard to put it all together. They had been trussed up and held prisoner, but had managed to escape, only to be caught and killed and left for the buzzards.

Fargo's lake blue eyes again turned to ice as they lingered a moment longer on the two young women. Both were reasonably young, probably once attractive before the buzzards had descended upon them. "Rest their souls," he muttered, cursing silently. He had nothing in his saddlebag with which to dig, but he took a moment to gather enough loose stones and broken branches to cover both young women's torn bodies. Finishing, he climbed onto the Ovaro and rode away, grateful for small victories, if only over a flock of vultures. He rode with his lips still pulled back in distaste, anxious to leave the spoiled and broken beauty, heading the pinto east across streams filled with leaping rainbow trout. The sun still bathed the high peaks of the Sangre de Christo Mountains when he came to a wide road. He followed it through a long valley until a town finally came into view.

He slowed as he drew closer to the town, seeing that it had taken on new dimensions. At the time of his last visit, years back, Bearsville had been a ragged place. Now it exuded an air of solidity with new buildings along the wide main street, a bank, an expanded general store, a barbershop, and a town meeting hall. He saw the usual freight wagons, Owensboro mountain wagons, and top-bowed Texas wagons, but he also noted a sprinkling of phaetons and surreys. Cowhands, prospectors with their tool-laden mules, along with well-dressed gentlemen walked the wide street. He was surprised only at how quickly Bearsville had sprung up. It was a town in a good place for growth. Men with money from Denver, Colorado Springs, and Cañon City could easily visit from the north, as could money from Santa Fe and Albuquerque in New Mexico to the south, not to mention all the newly prosperous miners and businessmen in between.

Fargo slowed as he came abreast of a large two-story building with bare-breasted maidens carved alongside the entrance doors. Gold letters marched across the top of the entranceway. BEARSVILLE EMPORIUM, he read and, in slightly smaller letters: GIRLS AND GAMBLING, FUN AND CULTURE. Fargo rode on as he noted that the second story of the building was circled with small windows. He'd gone on another few streets when he drew to a halt in front of a window sign that bore the single word: SHERIFF. His hand pressed the letter in his pocket, a reflex gesture. Hank Carlson had sent it and Hank didn't ask for help lightly. Fargo had agreed to visit as soon as he finished breaking trail for the Cole brothers in Kansas. Besides, he hadn't seen Hank in years. It was time for a reunion. Hank Carlson was a good sheriff when he was back in east Kansas, an honest and fair man. He was just as good a one in Colorado, Fargo was certain.

Dropping the Ovaro's reins over the hitching post, Fargo stepped into the sheriff's office. Two men immediately turned to him as he entered. It took him a long moment to recognize the one that rose. The Sheriff Hank Carlson he'd known had dark red hair, a ruddy complexion, full cheeks, and a strong face. The man before him was a study in gray, his face thin, cheeks sunken, hair wintry, skin the gray of old dust. Fargo tried not to let the shock show on his face and knew he'd not really succeeded as Hank Carlson came toward him. "Fargo, you made it. God, it's good to see you," the sheriff said and Fargo grasped a hand that had only half the strength he once knew.

"Got your letter. Came as soon as I could, Hank," Fargo said.

The man nodded and Fargo saw a sadness come into his face. "I'm not the man you knew, old friend, but you can see that," the sheriff said. "I'm sick, real sick." He turned to the other man. "This is Doc Berenson. He spends a lot of time with me, gives me enough pills to keep me doing my job as best I can," Hank Carlson said.

"I do whatever I can," the doctor said, rising, a tall, thin-faced man, balding with a narrow nose, steady eyes with a quiet competence to him. "Glad you could make it, Fargo. Hank's been counting off each day waiting for you." The sheriff turned away as Doc Berenson met Fargo's eyes, giving a helpless shrug that said volumes. Hank Carlson's voice broke Fargo's grimness.

"I'll be turning in my badge soon enough, Fargo," the man said.

"Got somebody to take it, Hank?" Fargo asked.

"An old acquaintance, Sam Walker. But he can't do it for another month, maybe two. There are a few things I have to take care of before that. One of them is sitting in the next room in a cell," the sheriff said. Gesturing for Fargo to follow him, they crossed to an adjoining room which was a six-by-eight-foot cell. A man sat on the edge of a narrow cot, a stringy figure with a foxlike face and small, darting eyes. "Freddie Steamer. He's a very special prisoner," the sheriff said. "He and his gang have made a career robbing over a dozen banks from Idaho to Iowa."

"He's the only one you caught?" Fargo questioned.

"We got lucky. He came here to visit a girlfriend and we got him. Been holding him ever since. His girl-friend pays him an occasional visit. I let her. I keep hoping she'll let something slip," Hank Carlson said. "I did learn that his gang is watching the town. That's why I called you. I'm supposed to deliver him to a Federal judge in Oklahoma."

"But you're not well enough to do it," Fargo guessed.

"That's only part of it. The other part is his gang is waiting and watching. Seems he's the only one who knows exactly where all their stolen money is hidden. I need someone to break a new trail out of here with him. I need you, Fargo," Hank Carlson said.

"Don't see where it'd be all that hard," Fargo said.

"It will be. There are places that give you cover every way out of Bearsville. His boys are at each of them, you can be sure. You're the only one who might break a trail past them. Will you do it for me, Fargo?" Hank Carlson asked.

"I'm here. Got nothing better to do," Fargo replied. Carlson offered a grateful smile as Fargo followed him from the room. The sheriff sank heavily into a chair behind the desk and Doc Berenson took Fargo aside.

"Thanks. That's better medicine than any I can give him," the doctor said.

"How long does he have?" Fargo asked, his voice hardly a whisper.

"Can't say for sure, except not long," the doc said

and Fargo swore silently as he went on to the front office. The sheriff rose as he came in, opened a desk drawer, and pulled out a star-shaped tin badge. He leaned forward and pinned it onto Fargo's shirt.

"No deputy's badge, not for you, Fargo," Hank Carlson said. "This town can stand two sheriffs, if only for a little while." He nodded toward the adjoining cell room. "When do you want to take him?" he asked.

"Tomorrow morning. I need a good night's sleep," Fargo said.

"I've extra rooms at my office," Doc Berenson offered.

"That'd be fine." Fargo nodded. "How many in Steamer's gang?" he asked Hank.

"Eight, but I'd guess they've hired some extra eyes," Hank said. "Remember, it's only after you've gone a ways out of town that they'll be watching. I don't know how you can get him through by day."

"Maybe I can't. I'll decide that in time," Fargo said when the door opened and a young girl entered, perhaps eighteen, Fargo guessed. A tight blouse made more of modest breasts than they deserved and Fargo took in her curvy, swinging hips. Her youthful face was attractive in a sullen, pouty way. Brown hair hung loose and long, and she carried a basket in one hand.

"Cooked some things for him," she announced belligerently, her eyes fastening on Hank Carlson. Fargo knew who she was at once. The sheriff took the basket from her, examined the contents, and handed it back to her. She raised her arms as he patted her down, searching for the bulge of a six-gun or derringer. "Enjoy yourself?" she tossed at him defiantly when he finished.

"Watch your mouth, girl," Carlson growled. "Go on

in." The girl hurried into the adjoining room, giving her hips an extra, obstinate sway. "Lola Carezza," Carlson said to Fargo.

"She just his girlfriend or part of his gang?" Fargo queried.

"Wish I knew. I'd arrest her if I had anything to charge her with," Hank said, lighting a lamp as night descended. "I'm running out of energy. That doesn't take long these days. But I'll have Steamer ready for you come morning."

He reached into the desk drawer, brought out an envelope and handed it to Fargo. "Official transfer papers for Steamer. For Judge Frederick Bolstrom, in Oklahoma City. Don't take Steamer lightly, Fargo. He knows there's a hangman's noose waiting for him when you deliver him to Judge Bolstrom."

"I never take desperate men lightly," Fargo said. "See you in the morning."

"Thanks again, old friend," Hank said.

"Glad to help," Fargo replied and followed Doc Berenson outside and down the street to a neat, white-painted building that bore the single word: CLINIC. A small barn behind the building let him stable the Ovaro and Fargo was shown to a room that was one of three in a row, all identical, each spare and neat, with a freshly made up hospital bed. He undressed in the moonlight from the window and stretched out on the bed, finding it firm but comfortable.

The visit hadn't been what he'd expected, a reunion that was bittersweet, at best. Yet he was not unhappy that he had come. It was a good feeling to do a favor for an old friend in bad times. The thought stayed, comforting him during a night of less than sound sleep. When morning came, he rose, washed, and dressed, and went outside to saddle the Ovaro. He had just finished when Doc Berenson came up to him. "I'll come back after I've delivered Steamer. Hope you can keep Hank going," Fargo said.

"I'll try. No promises, I'm afraid," the doctor said.

Fargo walked the short distance to the sheriff's office. A faded brown gelding stood tied to the hitching post.

"In here," Hank Carlson called out, and Fargo followed his voice into the adjoining cell room. Freddie Steamer sat with his hands tied behind his back, Hank Carlson holding a rifle on him. Steamer wore a high-crowned Stetson pushed back on his head. "He's all yours, Fargo," the sheriff said.

"Untie him," Fargo said as Hank Carlson's eyes grew wide.

"Untie him?" the sheriff frowned.

"I saw too many Indian pony prints on the way here. The Shoshone may give me more trouble than his friends. I want him able to stop quick when I tell him, and run if we have to. He'll need his hands to handle his horse. I don't want to lose my scalp along with his," Fargo said.

"Whatever you say," Hank said with faint disapproval as he untied Steamer's bonds. The man rubbed his wrists and Fargo noted the crafty smirk that flashed in his beady eyes.

"Outside," Fargo commanded and walked the man to the brown gelding. He watched Steamer swing onto the horse. The man's eyes cut to Fargo as he pulled himself onto the Ovaro.

"Not keeping your gun on me?" Steamer asked, sarcasm edging his voice.

Fargo smiled pleasantly. "No need to," he said.

"You think you're that fast?" Steamer sneered.

Fargo kept the smile on his face but his hand moved with the smoothness and speed of a diamondback's strike. The Colt fired the instant it cleared the holster and Freddie Steamer's hat blew from his head, a neat hole almost magically appearing in the crown. Steamer's mouth dropped open. "That answer you?" Fargo said softly. Steamer said nothing, but he swallowed hard. "Pick up your hat," Fargo ordered and the man swung from the gelding, retrieved his hat and returned to the saddle. "Ride," Fargo said, keeping a half pace behind the gelding.

He steered the Ovaro through town, casting a curious glance at the Bearsville Emporium as they passed. Two men were plastering signs on the outside of the building. One read: FAMOUS OPERA SINGER PERFORMS. COME LISTEN. Another read: CULTURE IN COLORADO. He half smiled as he rode from town, starting down the road into the wide valley. His eyes swept the thick forest that rose on both sides of the valley, mostly red cedar and hackberry with clusters of cottonwoods mingling with the open land in the center of the valley. Turning, he moved into the red cedar forest, staying among the trees as he slowly rode forward with his prisoner. Steamer rode quietly, nary a word from him, but Fargo didn't let the man's silence lull him into relaxing. Steamer was a desperate man who'd spend every minute looking for a chance to run. But he wouldn't take any wild risks, Fargo was certain. The hole in his hat was a reminder he'd not quickly forget.

Fargo peered into the trees, his eyes sweeping across the land, pausing at every slope and rise, looking for any movement of leaves or brush that was made not by nature but by man, alert to the subtle differences as only a trailsman or an Indian scout would note. With

12

each brand search he brought his eyes back to Steamer, taking in the way the man sat his horse, the tension in his posture, the deliberate set of his shoulders and hands. But he saw nothing to make him suspect Steamer was preparing to make a break for freedom. Instead, the man looked faintly uncomfortable, leaning forward in the saddle. Fargo returned to searching the distant trees and his next glance at Steamer showed the man looking more uncomfortable, both his hands now tightly gripping the saddle horn. Steamer lifted his eyes to look at Fargo, his lips pulled back in a grimace. "Got to stop," he breathed. "My stomach. It's killin' me."

"Your girlfriend's cooking?" Fargo asked wryly.

"Didn't eat anything else," Steamer said and groaned. "Let me off the damn horse . . . just for a few minutes."

They had been moving over uneven terrain, Fargo admitted, and nodded at Steamer's request. "Get off," he grunted, watching the man slide from the saddle and sink to the ground, bending over with his arms pressed to his stomach. "Don't do anything stupid," Fargo warned.

"I'm too busy hurtin'," Steamer muttered.

Fargo watched the man stay stooped over, both arms pressed against his midsection, his foxlike face drawn tight. Fargo didn't see anything tricky in the man's actions. On his knees, arms held to his stomach, Steamer was in no position to try and run or make any quick moves. Fargo took his eyes from the man and peered through the trees again, once more searching along the distant line of forests. He brought a quick glance back to Steamer and found the man had straightened up some, but was still on his knees. "Ready to ride?" Fargo asked.

"Just a few minutes more," Steamer said.

Fargo brought his gaze back to another sweep of the open land and the clusters of red cedar when, out of the corner of his eye, he caught the sudden movement of Steamer's arm. Snapping his gaze back to the man, he was just in time to see Steamer pulling the knife from inside his shirt. "Damn," Fargo bit out as Steamer flung the blade, a narrow, double-edged stiletto. The man's throw was fast and entirely too accurate as Fargo saw the knife hurtling at his stomach. Pressing on the stirrups, he pushed himself upward, lifting his body as he twisted away from the stiletto to try and take the blade someplace less fatal than his gut. Still clinging to the saddle, he knew he had managed to avoid the sharp, narrow knife plunging into his vitals as he felt the impact of the blade. A flash of gratefulness swept through him as he felt no sharp, sudden pain.

He yanked at the Colt to pull it from the holster, but the gun refused to come out. Glancing down at his side, he saw the hilt of the stiletto protruding from the holster. In a freak, ten-thousand-to-one chance, the stiletto had gone through the opening of the trigger guard of the revolver, deep into the other side of the holster where it was now imbedded. It became a barrier that wouldn't let him pull the Colt out of the holster, and he gave up trying after another two attempts to free the weapon. The sound of hoofbeats echoed through the air and he saw Freddie Steamer racing off on the brown gelding.

"Son of a bitch," Fargo growled as he sent the Ovaro into a gallop, seeing Steamer heading for the edge of the tree line to race into the open. At a light slap against his powerful, jet black neck, the Ovaro put his powerfully muscled hindquarters into play and, skirting trees, he closed ground quickly before Steamer's faded brown gelding could reach the forest's edge. The man turned the horse away, and tried escaping through the trees and found the Ovaro quickly cutting him off again. Steamer tried to turn, racing back behind Fargo to reach the treeline, but Fargo sent the pinto into a tight spin, coming abreast of the fleeing prisoner as open land rose up only a hundred feet away. He brought the Ovaro alongside the brown gelding, one arm raised to take the blow he expected Steamer would throw. But the man surprised him, flattening himself in the saddle and clinging to the horse now only a dozen yards from the open land.

Rising up in the stirrups once again, Fargo flung himself in a sideways dive and landed atop Steamer. Gripping onto the man, he fell from the horse with him, hitting the ground hard and hearing Steamer's breath fly from him. Rolling aside, Fargo pushed to his feet and looked at Freddie Steamer, who lay facedown, gasping for breath. He allowed the man another half-minute to recover the wind that had been knocked from him, and as Steamer started to regain his feet, Fargo slammed him against the trunk of a big red cedar. With a groan, Steamer slid down to his knees against the trees. Fargo stepped to the Ovaro, taking the lariat from its saddle strap.

Using the blade of the Arkansas toothpick in his calf-holster, he cut a length of the lariat and tied Steamer's hands in front of him. "Guess we'll do it Hank's way," Fargo muttered. The gelding had halted at the edge of the trees and Fargo brought the horse back, then pulled Steamer to his feet and pushed the man onto the gelding. Draping Steamer's hands atop the saddle horn, Fargo stepped back and reached one hand down to his holster, where his fingers curled around the smooth hilt of the stiletto. He had to yank hard before the blade came free of his holster. When it emerged, he turned the weapon in his fingers and saw how the narrow flatness could have been carried in by Lola without being detected, probably hidden in the waistband of her skirt. "She smuggle this to you yesterday?" Fargo asked Steamer.

"No," Steamer said sullenly. "I've been keeping it to use at the right time."

"Almost the right time," Fargo corrected, swinging onto the Ovaro and leading the way forward, shrouded by the tree cover again. He hadn't gone more than ten minutes more when he pulled to a halt. A sound filled the forest, a sound that seemed to make everything stop around them.

2

Fargo sat silently in the saddle, not moving a muscle. It seemed as if the entire forest listened with him. The trees became quiet, not a leaf rustling. The columbines lifted their heads. A red squirrel sat still as a stone as a soprano voice curled through the trees, a song of shimmering beauty that grew full with sensuous power, then diminished to caressing softness. Memory flowed back, drenching Fargo in another time and another place. He recognized the song . . . an aria from an Italian opera. But more information than that refused to come back to him, even as he shuffled frantically through the pages of his memory.

The aria ended but, after a moment, the young woman began to sing again, in French this time. She sang without accompaniment from somewhere in the forest not too far away. Fargo swung down from the saddle. He had held to one rule all his life: Never turn away from a beautiful moment. Always stop to smell the flowers, to watch a sunset, listen to a lark, admire a magnificent stallion or a beautiful woman. Beauty existed as a gift, to be enjoyed, savored. He saw no reason to change his ways, even now. Walking from the Ovaro, he pulled Freddie Steamer from the gelding. He took another piece of his lariat and tied the man's wrists to a length of tree branch, his arms extended upward.

"I'll be back," Fargo said.

"You just going to leave me hanging here?" Steamer protested.

"Be grateful I'm not the judge in Oklahoma," Fargo said and disappeared through the trees. He hurried through the forest, following the sound of the delightful singing, and had just spied a little cabin when the aria ended. He crept closer, and saw the cabin was set in a small hollow surrounded by red cedar. A buckboard stood alongside one wooden wall and just as Fargo stepped closer, the singing began again, filling the little hollow with glorious sound. The cabin door was open, he saw, but he couldn't pick out the singer. Leaning against the fragrant reddish brown bark of a cedar, he put his head back and closed his eyes as he listened. Entranced by the plaintive beauty of the music, a new sound that came to him was harshly intrusive as it broke into a rare moment. Fargo found himself instantly angry as he snapped his eyes open.

Peering through the trees, he saw six men pushing into the open door of the cabin. As they rushed in the singing broke off, a scream taking its place. Fargo bolted from the tree, dropping into a crouching run as he made for the side window in the cabin. Reaching the cabin, he peered over the sill of the window and saw the young woman inside the cabin's single room, one of the six men holding her roughly by the wrist. His quick glance at her showed her to have full, shiny black hair and flashing eyes to match, a handsome face with a straight nose and luscious lips. Full breasts threatened to billow over the top edge of a white, scoop-necked blouse. "Let go of me," she declared to the man holding her, a rough-faced character with a sharp nose.

"Little spitfire, ain't she?" one of the others said with a laugh.

The young woman's answer was another sudden effort that managed to pull her wrist free of the man's grip. "Don't make it harder for yourself, honey," the sharp-nosed one said.

"What do you mean?" the girl threw back.

"That was your last song, baby," the man said.

"What are you talking about?" She frowned.

"It's over. You're over," the man said.

The young woman stared at him, realization taking a moment to sink through her surprise and disbelief. "No, this is impossible. This isn't happening," she murmured.

"Guess again, girlie," one of the others said. The young woman exploded, whirling, darting past outstretched hands, avoiding another pair, her full, black hair streaming behind her. She had almost reached the door when one of the men tackled her, bringing her down. Fargo caught a glimpse of her long, lovely legs as she fell, trying to get up, kicking out at her attacker. But other hands yanked her to her feet and the sharp-nosed one flung his arms around her as two others held her down. He mashed her breasts upward with his chest as he cruelly pressed against her.

"Easy, honey. We're going to show you one last good time, first." He snickered. She struggled, trying to break away but she was helpless to move. Fargo felt the Colt in his hand, and raised the gun to the edge of the windowsill but held back firing. He could take down most of them with his first volley but most wasn't good enough. He cursed silently. He needed to prevent her from becoming a hostage and that was impossible with all of them clustered around her. The best chance was to force them out of the cabin and get some space between them and the girl. Dropping into a crouch again, he ran toward the edge of the trees where they had put their horses. As he did, the young woman's cries began to turn to screams, the men's laughter growing coarser. He reached the cluster of aspen and threw the horses' reins free, slapping his palm down hard against two rumps. The two horses bolted with a clatter of hooves, the others racing off with them.

The shouts from inside the cabin immediately changed in tone and seconds later Fargo saw figures running from the cabin door. But he was already on one knee inside the trees, the Colt raised as the men stared after the bolting horses. "What in hell got into them?" one rasped.

"Somethin' set them off," another said.

The sharp-nosed one came from the cabin, holding the young woman in front of him, his arms wrapped around her waist. "Go get them, for Christ's sake!" he ordered. As the others started to run after the horses, the young woman helped herself more than she realized. Trying to tear away from her captor, she twisted her body and kicked backward, raking her heel down the man's calf. "Goddamn," he cursed, throwing her to the ground. "Bitch," he roared. But he no longer had her in front of him and Fargo, now with a clear shot, fired. The man's sharp-nosed face seemed to grow sharper as the shot hit, the skin pulling even tighter around his face in a painful grimace. He did a tiny dancelike step before collapsing in a heap.

But Fargo had already swung the Colt in a half circle as the other five skidded to a halt, yanking their guns out as surprise seized their faces. Fargo fired again and two went down in a tangle of arms and legs as they fell into one another. A fourth one fired off one shot before Fargo's next bullet blew him backward into a tall bush of coralberry. The last two fired wildly in the general direction from which Fargo's shots had come, running as they did. They disappeared into the trees and he traced their flight by the sounds of their crashing through the brush and leaves. He waited, heard the footsteps slow when they caught up to their horses, and holstering the Colt, he stepped from the trees. He hurried to where the young woman lay trembling against the cabin, her coal black eyes round with shock.

He pulled her to her feet and she clung to him, her warm softness pressing into him. "It's over," he said quietly and she finally pushed back a step to stare up at him. Despite the ordeal she had experienced, he saw eyes that held more fire than fear.

"Who are you?" she asked.

"Name's Fargo . . . Skye Fargo," he said.

"Andrea Kalistro," she said.

Fargo glanced at the figures scattered on the ground. "Who were they?" he asked.

"I don't know. I haven't any idea," Andrea Kalistro said.

"Or why they came after you?" Fargo asked.

"No, none at all. I don't understand any of this, none of it at all, but I'm going to find out," Andrea Kalistro said, her eyes flashing angrily. She could turn quickly from softly sweet to fiery imperiousness. He saw she had a mercurial quality to her.

"How do you figure to find out?" Fargo asked.

"I'm going into town to talk to Bartley Haskell. He knows everything that goes on around here. Besides, he's the man who hired me and brought me out here."

She put her hands on his chest. "Will you go back with me? I've no right to ask, after all you've just done for me, but two of them got away."

"I'd guess they're still running," Fargo said but he understood the apprehensiveness in her dark eyes. She was a stranger to this land and its sudden eruptions of violence. He'd go back with her. Getting Freddie Steamer to Oklahoma could wait another day. Besides, he was curious why they had attacked her in the first place. "All right," he told Andrea. "But I'll have to bring somebody along, a prisoner I'm taking to Oklahoma."

"You're a sheriff?" Andrea asked with a frown.

"For the moment," he said. He rose and her lips brushed his cheek, her deep breasts soft against his chest.

"Thank you, Fargo. You are proof," she said softly.

"Of what?"

"That a real knight doesn't need shining armor," she finished.

"Hitch up your buckboard while I go get my prisoner." He smiled, and strode to the Ovaro and made his way back to where he had left Freddie Steamer. When he reached the spot, he felt the curse well up inside him. The brown gelding was gone. So was Freddie Steamer. "Damn," Fargo bit out and swung to the ground, stepping to the branch where he had tied his prisoner. It had been broken off, he saw, and he swore again as he began to examine the remaining section. The broken end of the branch showed that it had been thoroughly dried out, its brittleness concealed by its tough bark. The rest was easy enough to put together. Unable to untie himself, Freddie Steamer had used the time and the commotion of the attack on the cabin to

22

frantically pull on the branch until it broke, no doubt surprising him. Fargo's eyes swept the ground. The other part of the branch was missing. It was with Freddie Steamer as, still unable to untie his wrists, he had pulled himself onto the gelding along with the branch and raced away.

Fargo swore again, at himself this time. A combination of circumstances had abetted his escape. First, his decision to stop and enjoy the singing. That would have posed no problem in itself had the attackers not appeared. They had provided Freddie Steamer with the time and the noise to cover his desperate efforts. Lastly, and perhaps most importantly, the bark had thoroughly concealed the branch's fragility. It had all added up to disaster and an escaped bank robber. Fargo knew there was no avoiding his blame in the matter and saw no reason not to return to Bearsville. He'd keep his promise to Hank and try to get a lead on Steamer from the girl. Lola Carezza had to know more than she professed. It was time to find out.

When Fargo returned to the cabin, Andrea Kalistro was waiting in the buckboard and he swung alongside her. "Where's your prisoner?" she asked.

"Gone. Vamoosed. Bad turn of luck." Fargo grimaced and rode beside the buckboard as the young woman sent the wagon forward with a snap of the reins. "You said this man Bartley Haskell hired you. For what? Tell me about yourself. I only know two things about you."

"And what are those?"

"You sing like an angel and you're not from around here," he said. She smiled with a certain loftiness, as though the compliment was appreciated yet hardly enough praise.

23

"You apparently know good singing when you hear it," Andrea said. "Where'd you learn?"

"I don't really. I just know something beautiful when I come on it, whether it's a song or a sunset," he said.

"A touch of the poet, too. How delightful." She smiled, her glance taking in the handsomeness of the Trailsman's chiseled features.

"This man Bartley Haskell, does he own the Bearsville Emporium?" Fargo asked.

"Yes, he wants to bring culture out here, he said. He wanted an opera star, and I've sung all over Europe," Andrea said.

"The first aria you sang, I heard it before but I can't put a name on it," Fargo said.

" 'Cara nome' . . . darling name, from Rigoletto, by Verdi."

"And the second . . . French, wasn't it?" Fargo queried.

"Yes, Bizet, from his *Pearl Fishers*."

"The third one was from another Italian opera?"

"Yes, Donizetti . . . *Lucia di Lammermoor,*" Andrea said.

"This going to be the first time you've sung out here?" Fargo asked.

"Yes," she said.

"You nervous about it?" he inquired, assuming she'd naturally have some apprehension.

"Not at all," she said haughtily. "I'm never nervous about performing. A good soprano should never be. Audiences will respond properly, whether they're musically educated or not."

"Folks respond differently out here," Fargo grunted.

"Nonsense. An audience is an audience," Andrea Kalistro pronounced imperiously. He didn't answer but wondered how many audiences she'd sung before

24

that packed six-guns. He thought back to a troop of acrobats and jugglers playing before an audience of miners that didn't like their performance. They weren't booed off the stage but were sent running for the wings in a hail of gunfire. He glanced at the young woman, at the defiant tilt of her chin, and decided she might do many things, but running wouldn't be one of them.

"Andrea Kalistro's not a name I've ever come on," he said.

"It's Italian and Greek, a perfect combination for a soprano," she said as she steered the buckboard onto a narrow road that hardly left room for him to ride alongside.

"What do you know about Bartley Haskell?" Fargo queried.

"Nothing, really, but he seems a genuine impresario and he's paying me very well," Andrea said. Fargo soon saw the buildings of the town rise up before them. Andrea steered through a crush of wagons and pulled up in front of the Bearsville Emporium. Fargo saw her take in the posters that had been plastered on the building walls, her picture on each of them.

"Disappointed?" Fargo asked quietly.

"I'm always disappointed in the ordinary publicity shots," she said dismissively. As she swung down from the buckboard, he watched the fullness of her breasts push up over the top of her neckline. His eyes weren't the only ones that followed her to the doorway, he noted. But it wasn't just because of her full figure and handsome face. She had a way to her that almost demanded attention and for the first time, he really understood the term *prima donna*. He caught up to her as she entered the Bearsville Emporium, seeing a large hall with a long bar against one wall, and rows

25

upon rows of chairs facing a curtained stage. Four open doorways led from the main floor to stairs that climbed to the second floor of the impressive structure.

A man came through one of the doorways, a large figure a little on the portly side. Gray sideburns framed a ruddy face that seemed amiable enough except for eyes that were hard as flint. He wore an expensive light blue jacket with an off white cravat and a diamond stickpin. "Andrea," the man said in surprise, his eyes flicking to Fargo. "What brings you here at this hour?"

"My friend, Skye Fargo," she introduced. "Bartley Haskell." Haskell allowed a polite nod. "Six men came to my cabin, saying they were going to kill me. Fargo stopped them," Andrea went on.

"Good God," Bartley Haskell exclaimed with a frown. "What a terrible thing."

"I want to know why. Who'd do such a thing?" Andrea questioned.

Bartley Haskell glanced at Fargo. "Andrea's not imagining their intentions?" he asked him.

"Nope," Fargo said and recounted what had happened. When he finished, Bartley Haskell scowled back.

"My God, I didn't think he'd stoop this low," the man murmured, awe in his voice.

"Who?" Andrea snapped.

"Emery Crater, of course. He runs the Bearsville Casino at the far end of town. He's always trying to go me one better. I heard he even hired his own opera singer," Haskell said.

"Really? Who?" Andrea broke in.

"An Ulla Stenson. She's from Europe, like you," Haskell said.

"That cow?" Andrea snorted. "She's hardly in my class."

"All the more reason for him to get rid of you. He didn't want me to have a genuine opera star, especially one that's better than his."

"That's a mighty strong accusation. You have any proof to back it up?" Fargo said.

"Proof? Hell, putting two and two together is proof enough. Who else stands to gain by getting rid of my star attraction? He's the only one. Common sense is proof enough," Bartley Haskell returned.

Fargo turned the man's words over in his mind. His simple logic was compelling, he had to admit. "You boys are into ruthless competition," Fargo said.

"We live or die by getting audiences in," Haskell replied.

"What if he tries again?" Andrea cut in.

"I'll have a man stand guard at the cabin," Haskell said. "But I doubt he'll try it again. He knows we'll be ready now. Besides, we'll be opening in a few days. It'll be too late, then. You'll already be singing."

"Still, I'm frightened," Andrea said.

"I'll go have a talk with this Emery Crater," Fargo said, and Andrea's arms encircled his neck.

"Would you? I'd feel so much better," she murmured and again he felt the undeniable softness of her breasts against his chest.

"I'll stop at the cabin tonight, give you my take on it," Fargo said.

She kissed his cheek. He felt the warm wetness of her lips as they lingered for just a moment longer than they needed to. "I'll be waiting," she breathed.

"He was behind it. Take my word for it. He's a rotten son of a bitch," Bartley Haskell said. Fargo saw his glance rest on the badge pinned to his shirt as Andrea stepped back. "You the one taking over for Hank Carlson?" Haskell asked. "I heard talk."

"For now," Fargo said.

"You get rid of Emery Crater and this'll be a much better town," Haskell exclaimed. Fargo kept the smile inside himself. Perhaps Haskell was right, but he also seemed too quick to seize on a chance to get rid of his competition.

"There's some cleaning up needed at Andrea's cabin. Send a wagon," Fargo said.

"Right away," Haskell nodded.

"While I'm here I'll do some practicing on stage," Andrea said as Fargo strode away. Outside, he didn't seek out Emery Crater's place. There were other things he had to do first. When he arrived at the sheriff's office he was greeted by a piece of paper tacked to the door.

"Want Sheriff Carlson? Go to Doc Berenson's," he read aloud, then turned and walked to the white-painted building. Doc Berenson rose from a chair to greet him, his thin face mirroring surprise.

"Fargo! You're the last person I expected to come calling," the doc said.

"Me too," Fargo said grimly. "Freddie Steamer escaped. Part my fault, part plain bad luck. Where's Hank? I want to tell him and get some questions answered before I go after Steamer."

"He's had a real bad session. I don't want to wake him. Sleep is vital for him. Besides, he hears this and it could send him into another attack," Doc Berenson said. "Maybe I can answer things for you. Hank talked about everything with me."

"I want to know where Steamer's girl is staying," Fargo said.

"At the hotel, a few streets down. She's been there ever since Hank put Steamer behind bars," the doctor said. "You thinking she'll lead you to him?"

"Maybe. Or he'll send someone to fetch her to him. Either way, I want to be there," Fargo said.

"How do you figure to watch her twenty-four hours a day, or don't you sleep?" Doc Berenson asked.

"I'll need help. I'd thought Hank could come along," Fargo said.

"Not now he can't. He'd be lucky to stay awake for fifteen minutes at a time," the doc said.

"You know anybody I can use, and trust?" Fargo asked.

Doc Berenson pondered for a moment. "Only one person. Willie Whitten. But he's the town drunk. Whiskey Willie, they call him."

"No thanks. I want someone reliable, someone I can count on," Fargo said.

"Strangely enough, Willie Whitten would be more reliable than anybody else. Of course, you'd have to sober him up first. But he'd stay off the bottle if he knew it was for Hank. They've had a special relationship for years. Hank's been a real friend to Willie, the only friend he has in town, and Hank's the only person he really respects. I'd give it a try," the doc said.

"You're really saying I don't have much choice," Fargo grumbled.

"Comes out to that," the doctor said. "Especially if you want somebody you can trust. Willie's a drunk but he has his own brand of integrity that he sticks to."

"Maybe that's why he drinks," Fargo commented. "Where do I find him?"

"He's got a shack a quarter mile past the south end of town."

"All right. I'll be stopping by again," Fargo said and abruptly left the quiet of the clinic. Outside, he led the Ovaro through the town until he found the hotel, a narrow, clapboard structure that edged seediness. Freddie Steamer was no doubt still running, trying to meet up with his friends, but Fargo wanted to assure himself about Lola Carezza. He halted at the hotel and went inside, where a sallow-faced young man looked up from inside a cubicle just past the doorway. Room keys hung on a pegboard at his back, an open registry ledger rested in front of him. "Lola Carezza," Fargo simply said.

"Room eight, second floor," the youth said in a bored tone.

"She out or in?" Fargo asked.

"I don't keep track," the youth replied.

Fargo nodded, turned, and strode from the hotel, aware the clerk watched him with one eyebrow lifted. Once outside, Fargo slipped around to the back of the building where, as he expected, he found a rear door. It was left open and as he entered, he halted and glanced down a long corridor that led to the front desk. The staircase that led up to the second floor was uncomfortably near the desk, Fargo noted as he crept forward. Reaching the bottom of the stairs, his eyes cut to the front desk again. The clerk was not visible, obviously seated out of view in his cubicle. Moving in a half crouch, Fargo swung himself around the bottom baluster of the staircase and took the steps two at a time. At the top, he found a short, dim hallway, the room he was looking for at the far end of it.

Pressing his ear to the door, he listened intently and heard no sounds from the other side. Still, he realized, she could be quietly sleeping, and he carefully tried the doorknob, finding it locked. Drawing the narrow,

30

double-edged throwing knife from his calf-holster, he carefully slid the point of the blade in between the door and the jamb. The lock mechanism was a simple one, and he worked the toothpick's blade carefully and silently until he felt the lock give and the door unlatch. He pushed his head into the room, only to find it empty, and stepped inside. It was a small room with fading paint, furnished with a single bed against one wall and a battered dresser. Lola Carezza's clothes were scattered about the room and he quickly examined her things, delving into a travel bag, but finding nothing to help him track down Freddie Steamer.

But he saw what he had come to see. The girl had nothing packed. She was waiting, not about to take off at a moment's notice, and that's all he really wanted to assure himself of. There was time enough for him to do the things he had to do, one of which was to find Willie Whitten. But first, he'd keep his promise to Andrea. He crossed the room in three long strides, slipped into the hall, and closed the door after him. He quietly crept down the stairs, and seeing that the desk clerk was still inside his cubicle, Fargo darted around the bottom baluster and down the corridor. Once outside the rear door, he led the pinto through the town until he came to a large, square structure, almost a duplicate in size to Bartley Haskell's emporium. As with Haskell's place, the entire second floor seemed to consist of small rooms with individual windows. Large gold letters over the entranceway proclaimed: BEARSVILLE CASINO—BIGGEST AND BEST.

Below, on the ground-floor windows, Fargo saw posters picturing a fresh-faced young woman with short, blond hair, wide-set blue eyes, and a frank, open expression. Though she looked nothing like Andrea, there was a sameness to the upward tilt of her chin, he noted. Fargo hitched the pinto and started to enter the casino when three men appeared. One seemed to be a veritable walking tree, at least seven feet tall, Fargo guessed—a thin, angular figure with a face to match, long-jawed, long-nosed, with flat facial features. Only the small, slitted, hard blue eyes didn't fit the long lines of the rest of his face. A shock of thick, black hair topped his elongated head. The man blocked his path as the other two took their places beside him, looking more like obedient little boys than men beside his hulking figure.

"Come to see Emery Crater," Fargo said.

"Got to check your gun," the towering figure said in a voice as deep as it was tall.

"Name's Fargo. I'm acting sheriff for Hank Carlson," Fargo said.

"Makes no difference. Mr. Crater's rules. No guns inside the casino. Can't let you in with it," the man said adamantly. "Sheriff Carlson always checked his gun when he visited."

Fargo's eyes narrowed. There was no way to verify the man's assertion on the spot, and he didn't like the idea of turning over his gun. There was a strangely menacing quality to the towering giant. Yet he didn't come for a confrontation. Fargo pondered, cursing silently at decisions that seemed harmless. Yet he had seen too many that had often turned out very differently.

"Who might you be?" Fargo asked the walking tree.

"Clay Beemis. I'm Mr. Crater's right hand," the man said. "You get your gun back when you leave."

Fargo swore again as he lifted the Colt from its holster. If it was the custom and Hank had gone along with it, he wouldn't make an issue, but he felt a wave of uneasiness as he handed Clay Beemis the gun. Beemis pushed the gun at one of the other men and led the way into the casino, where Fargo took in a large auditorium, with a stage at one side. A young woman stood on the stage and Fargo recognized her from the posters outside. She was larger in person than she seemed on the posters, her face fuller, her hair a reddish blond. Deep breasts pushed out against a green shirt and Fargo took in her full figure, ample hips, and a deep rib cage, yet she carried everything well, every part of her firm and supple. She stepped to where an upright piano stood, a slight-built figure seated at the keyboard.

The first notes tinkled from the piano, and then she began to sing in a powerful voice, much larger than Andrea's, with notes that spiraled to the ceiling. He listened, enthralled by the thrilling power of her voice, power with beauty, crystal-clear notes that curled around every corner of the auditorium. He'd heard enough German to recognize the language, but the music was unfamiliar. Yet its beauty held him spellbound and when she turned to fully face him from the stage, he saw her sparkling blue eyes, even, attractive features, a short nose, and full, pink cheeks. Even in song, her mouth was large, her hips very full. Her very deep breasts lifted and fell as she sang, straining against the fabric of her emerald blouse, pressing two sizeable points into the material.

When she finished the song, a man stepped from behind the stage curtain, applauding as he did. "Magnificent, my dear, truly magnificent," he gushed. The young woman's smile was regally gracious as the man turned, seeing Fargo waiting. "It seems we have an audience," the man said. "Did you like my opera star?" he asked Fargo.

"Very much," Fargo replied earnestly.

The young woman's sparkling blue eyes held a hint of mischief as they focused on him. "Ever heard an opera singer before?" she asked him.

"Yes," Fargo said. "Surprised?"

The young woman laughed. "Yes, but a lot of things out here surprise me. It's a place of contrasts, terrible beauty and terrible harshness, brutality and kindness. I'm Ulla Stenson, from Sweden."

"Skye Fargo," he said.

"When did you hear an opera singer?" Ulla Stenson asked.

"Once, a few years back, then I heard Andrea Kalistro today."

The young woman tossed a chiding glance at him. "I thought you said you'd heard an *opera* singer. Andrea tries. That's the most I can say for her. Come to hear

34

my performance. Then you'll *really* hear an opera singer."

Fargo nodded. It was plain that Ulla was as opinionated as Andrea. "I'll try." He nodded and Clay Beemis broke in, irritation clear in his voice.

"He came to see you, Mr. Crater," Beemis said to Crater.

"I'll be going back to the cabin," Ulla said to Crater and swept past him only to pause at the door, her sparkling blue eyes finding Fargo. "Don't forget to come hear me. We can talk afterwards. I didn't know there was such a thing as a cowboy opera fan. I'm fascinated."

"Didn't say I was a fan, just that I've heard opera," Fargo corrected.

"No matter. Just come listen. You'll hear what good singing is," Ulla Stenson said and hurried outside. She dispensed the same imperiousness Andrea did, he noted with quiet amusement. Turning to Emery Crater, he saw a man who liked tailored suits and cravats as much as Bartley Haskell. He also had the same expansiveness but on a tighter, small-mouthed face, his nose thin with a sight twist, as though it might have once been broken. Fargo decided to be blunt.

"Somebody tried to kill Andrea Kalistro, the opera singer Bartley Haskell hired," Fargo began. "There's talk that maybe you were behind it."

"Talk? That kind of talk could only have come from Bartley Haskell himself," the man said indignantly. "He'd be the only one who'd accuse me of such nonsense."

"I won't go into that, but talk is that you're the only one stands to gain from getting rid of the girl," Fargo said evenly.

Clay Beemis stepped forward, his long face darkening. "You accusing us, mister?" he asked.

"I'm not accusing anybody. I'm just saying I don't want any more of it. Look at it as friendly advice," Fargo said.

"I look at it as accusing." The giant growled.

"You're wrong. A general warning, overall advice, that's all," Fargo said.

"It's accusing and I'm not standing still for it, Mr. Sheriff," Beemis said with dripping sarcasm in his voice.

Fargo glanced at Emery Crater. "You want to explain the difference between advice and an accusation to him?" he suggested.

"Can't do that. Clay's very easily upset and there's no turning him off when he gets that way." Emery Crater shrugged.

Fargo's eyes hardened. "Especially when you don't want to," he said. Crater didn't answer.

"You need a lesson, Mr. Sheriff. You need to learn about who runs this town," Clay Beemis said. Fargo saw the other two men step back, one locking the front door to the casino. He saw Emery Crater turn away and Fargo swore inwardly as he remembered the unease he'd felt when he gave up his Colt. He took a step backward as the treelike figure started toward him.

"Time for your lesson." Beemis sneezed, his long arms swaying at his sides. Fargo's glance took in the auditorium, the chairs placed in neat rows, the raised platform of the stage behind the chairs, and the open space in front. Fargo tensed, letting the man draw closer. He halted suddenly, then shot out a left hook and was surprised how quickly one of Beemis's long arms came up to parry the blow. The next surprise was even more unpleasant when Fargo found that the man's arms were even longer than they seemed. And much faster. Beemis shot out a straight left and though Fargo managed to partly duck away, he felt the man's power as his bludgeoning blow sideswiped his ribs. Fargo danced away, then started to come in again, feinting and throwing two punches. Beemis parried both with his long arms, launching his own flurry of blows. Fargo sidestepped all of them, trying to counter, and failed to reach the man's head, finding himself ducking away from another series of powerful punches.

Fargo was in a half crouch when Beemis suddenly leaped, his long arms outstretched, the move surprising in its unexpectedness and speed. Fargo twisted his body away but felt the man's arms close around his legs. He tried to kick away but Clay Beemis pulled, pitching Fargo forward, Beemis's arms still clamped around his legs. Suddenly, Fargo was lifted by his legs and flung into the air as though he were a rag doll. He sailed across open space, bringing his arms up over his face as he went crashing into the first row of chairs.

He heard chair legs breaking and wood splintering as he landed, but the seats helped to stop him from smashing his head against the unyielding floor. He lay there for a moment, pushing aside pieces of chair when he heard Clay Beemis thundering toward him. Fargo rolled as a giant foot crashed down inches from his head. He reached out to grab hold of one elephantine leg. He yanked at the man's knee in order to upend the giant, but his leg was as if it were rooted in the ground. It didn't budge. Fargo cursed as he rolled away, but a pile driver blow hammered down on his back. He gasped in pain but forced himself to keep rolling, barely avoiding another back-breaking blow. Shaking his head to clear it, he pushed to his feet, seeing Clay Beemis's towering figure charging at him.

Fargo gave ground, then ducked and spun away as Beemis charged past him. Swinging a short, hard hook, Fargo drove his fist into the small of Beemis's broad back and had the satisfaction of hearing the man grunt in pain. Fargo stepped in and tried another blow at Beemis's jaw, but the man swept one long arm backward and Fargo's punch bounced harmlessly aside. Beemis turned to face him and Fargo feinted, ducking low and launching another punch, punching upward at the man's head. The blow fell short so he followed with a right that missed as Beemis pulled his head back. Clay Beemis countered with a swarming attack, one sweeping, roundhouse blow after another. Fargo tried to slip punches in between them but had to fall back in defense as he saw it was not unlike trying to push through between the blades of a windmill in a gale.

Beemis, a gargoyle's grin curling his lips, leaped in with another flurry. Fargo was forced to retreat. Split-second decisions flashed through his mind. Beemis was simply too tall, the vulnerability of his jaw out of reach. Fargo realized he had to try a different tactic. A lumberjack out to bring down a tree doesn't start chopping at the top, he realized as he danced away from another of Beemis's charges. He went into a crouch as Beemis weaved forward, avoiding a blow and coming in low. This time, Fargo's fists smashed into the man's long midsection. Beemis gasped and halted in his tracks.

Fargo feinted and the towering figure threw two wild punches. Fargo came under each and drove another powerful blow into the man's midsection. Beemis wheezed for air and this time he sagged, bending over. Fargo then brought up a whistling uppercut that landed flush on the man's jaw. A followup left drove deep into Beemis's solar plexus. Again, the towering figure doubled over and again Fargo smashed another right to the man's jaw. Beemis fell sideways, struggling up on one knee, his jaw hanging open limply. Fargo stepped in for another blow, and realized too late that he had grown confident too quickly. One long arm swept out, slamming into his calves, and Fargo felt himself go down. Powerful arms encircled his legs again, but this time he kicked free, crawling and stumbling forward into the smashed chairs. He was trying to get to his feet when a swift kick smashed into him, catapulting him forward across the broken chairs. Wincing as splinters of chair dug into him, Fargo pushed onto his knees.

Grunting in pain, he felt himself knocked sideways, and he landed on his back amidst the litter of chairs once again. He looked up to see the imposing man in midair, coming down at him like a falling redwood. There was no time to roll or twist away to avoid being crushed by the weight and power of the falling behemoth. Fargo saw Clay Beemis's mouth pulled back in a silent roar of triumph and then, his hand closing around the jagged broken leg of a chair, Fargo pulled the stump to him, using every last ounce of his strength to hold it up. His body quivered in shock as he saw Clay Beemis impale himself onto the jagged length of broken chair leg. A shower of red exploded from Beemis's chest as the chair drove deep through shattered bone, torn tissue, and skin. Beemis slumped over him, his breath a strangled, bubbling sound.

Fargo raised his knees and pushed the now-limp figure off to one side.

Fargo glanced at Beemis, who lay still, the chair leg embedded in his chest, a pool of crimson oozing out from around the piece of wood. Emery Crater stepped closer, grimacing. Fargo walked across the front of the auditorium to where the other two men waited, fear in their eyes. Trying not to show how much his body throbbed and ached, he stopped before one of the men and held out his hand. The man gave Fargo back his Colt.

"Wise move," Fargo muttered, holstering the gun and turning to Emery Crater. "Don't forget my advice," he said.

"Wouldn't think of it," Crater replied. Fargo walked from the casino, slowly pulling himself onto the Ovaro as dusk began to settle over the town. He drew a deep breath and fought off a wave of pain that washed through his body. The Ovaro slowly moved forward, aware of its rider's pain and weakness owing to that special bond that existed between them. When the horse made its way out of town, Fargo guided it through the stands of aspen and as darkness fell, he reached the cabin. He saw the guard standing off to one side as he slowly eased himself from the saddle. Andrea heard him as he arrived, and hurried out to meet him. Her black eyes peered at him, seeing the pain in his face.

"You're hurt. What happened?" she asked.

"Emery Crater's man decided the town would be better off without me. Turned out to be the other way around," Fargo said but her eyes told him she understood without the need for further words. "There won't be anyone bothering you anymore but I'd say

Haskell was right about Crater," Fargo told her. Fishing into the saddlebag, he took out a staghorn bottle and she frowned at it. "Got to do some repair work," he said. She held his arm, leading him toward her cabin. Once inside, he had a chance to survey the room for the first time, seeing pillows strewn on the floor, an icebox in one corner, a luncheon table and a large bed with a blue cotton ticking blanket thrown over it. He eased himself down on the edge of the bed and began to take off his clothes.

Andrew went to the door and called to the guard. "You can go. Fargo will be staying," she said and closed the door. Fargo had his Levi's off when she turned back to him. The staghorn bottle was unstoppered and he was about to apply the salve to his body. "Let me do that," Andrea said, taking the bottle from him, pressing him down onto the bed. He turned on his stomach and she began to massage the soothing salve across his back. "What is this?" she asked.

"Birch bark compress, hyssop, balm of Gilead and mugwort. Damn good ointment for bruises and muscle injuries," Fargo muttered as he drank in the feel of her hands massaging him. She had a touch both firm and gentle and he felt the sore places all over his body begin to relax. "You're good. You do this often?" he asked.

"No. Like singing, it's a natural talent," she said.

"Speaking of singing, I heard Ulla Stenson," Fargo remarked.

"I hope you're not going to compare her to me," Andrea said, her voice instantly bristling, as her fingers dug into him.

"I wouldn't do that but she sounded fine to me," Fargo said carefully.

"Because you don't understand voices," Andrea said.

"That's for sure," Fargo agreed.

"She's a dramatic soprano, a big, heavy voice. But she keeps trying to sing Violetta, Tosca, Lucia. She even tries Norma," Andrea scoffed.

"That's bad?"

"It's pitiful. Those are roles for lyric soprano, a voice with lightness, agility, suppleness, and tender beauty, not a big, inflexible voice," Andrea snapped.

"If you say so," Fargo commented amiably.

She paused to peer at him. "I'll put it in terms you can understand. Would you use a Clydesdale to rope cattle? Of course not, because they wouldn't be agile enough, quick enough, or flexible enough."

"Point taken. I'm impressed," Fargo said.

"Besides, she's not even a very good dramatic soprano." Andrea sniffed. Fargo knew silence was his best reply, as he realized that he'd get no unbiased opinions from Andrea. He turned onto his back and she rubbed the ointment into his chest. When she finished, she didn't stop moving her hands across his chest and he saw her eyes rove over the chiseled muscles of his chest, her lips slightly parted. He also watched the steady rise and fall of her voluminous breasts as they kept expanding over the top of the scoop-necked blouse with each breath.

"Singing is such a sensual thing, perhaps the most sensual of all forms of music," she said. "It's the most direct of all musical expression. You are your instrument." Her hands continued to rub his chest, her touch beginning to stir him as he saw a tiny smile edge her lips.

"What are you thinking?" he asked.

"How long it takes for this salve to work." she answered.

"I ought to be myself in the morning," he said.

The little smile took on a new note of satisfaction. "I was given some sandwiches. They're in the icebox. Join me?" she said.

"That'd be good," Fargo said and sat up as Andrea fetched the sandwiches and two tin cups of cold water.

"Sorry, this is all I can offer," she said.

"It's fine," he said and sat up as Andrea positioned herself beside him. "How come Haskell doesn't have you stay in one of those rooms he has on the second floor instead of all the way out here alone?" Fargo questioned.

"They're strictly for the dancing girls. He realizes an opera singer is special," Andrea said.

"Guess Emery Crater feels the same way about his opera singer," Fargo said. "He's got her stashed away in a cabin, too."

"Well, we're hardly to be lumped in with dance girls," Andrea said. Fargo smiled. There were no pretensions about her loftiness. It was a built-in regality. Or perhaps it was simply part of being a soprano, he considered.

"I've a bedroll on my horse. I'll get it," he said as they finished the meal.

"Nonsense. You'll sleep in the bed, get a good night's rest," Andrea said, leaning down and turning off the lamp. Fargo pushed himself back onto the bed and listened to the rustle of silk and cotton as she undressed. He felt the bed move as she climbed in, settling down, keeping space between them. "Good night," she said firmly.

"You counting on my self-discipline?" he jested her.

43

"No, on your aches and pains," she said and he smiled at the answer's accuracy. As he closed his eyes, his body instantly pulled sleep around him. Exhaustion held him in a deep grip and he didn't wake until morning slipped through the cabin window. He glanced beside him. Andrea was a round bundled shape under the cover, sleeping soundly, so he slid quietly from the bed and went outside, and found a small well near the cabin. The soreness was gone from his body and, using a cloth from his saddlebag, he washed the salve from himself with well water, letting the morning sun beam down on him before returning to the cabin. Andrea was up, clothed in a short nightshirt of gray cotton. He saw the basin of water on the dresser and the wetness of her hair as she turned to him. Her eyes went to his bare chest, glistening with the water still on his body. When he came over to her, she pressed both hands against his muscled pectorals, her touch warm and soft.

Stepping back, she shrugged her shoulders and the straps of her nightshirt fell away. Another shrug and the garment dropped entirely to the floor. Deep, full breasts faced him, her Mediterranean background reflected in their light olive skin. Very round, very pert, their deepness pillowy, each olive-skinned, luscious mound was tipped by a large nipple, brown suffused with pink and encircled by an equally large areola of lighter brown. Below her breasts, he took in a waist a little thick yet not without a fleshy salacity. A round abdomen followed, very full with its own definitive sensuality. Below, a luxuriant V-shaped jet black tuft invited one's hands to explore its pleasures. The legs that followed were full, thighs well fleshed yet rippling with a bold, challenging sensuousness.

Everything about Andrea challenged the world, he decided, from the fire of her black eyes to the opulence of her ripe figure. "You being grateful?" he asked.

"No, you wouldn't want that. It wouldn't be your way," she said.

"Bull's-eye," he said with some surprise.

"A woman knows those things, feels them, senses them. You're like this country. There's a deep integrity at its core, beneath all the harshness." She paused, a tiny speculative smile edging her lips. "You know, someday some composer is going to write an opera about this America, this Wild West, with a soprano and tenor in the leading roles, of course." She laughed.

"This your way of preparing for the role?" He smiled.

"Why not? But right now it's my way of wanting," she said, her voice lowering to a husky whisper. She came forward, her large, firm breasts very soft as they pressed against his chest. He lay back on the bed and she stayed with him, her lips coming to his, moist and warm. Her mouth opened for him, her tongue darting forward immediately, a sweet harbinger of other senses, a messenger of pleasure. He locked mouths with her as her full-fleshed body rubbed against him, and he enjoyed the warm smoothness of her. Finally, tearing his lips from hers, he brought them down to one full breast, caressing its olive-skinned, silken smoothness. "Yes, oh, yes," Andrea breathed as he gently pulled on the large brown-pink nipple, tracing a path around the light brown areola, his tongue tasting every sweet edge. Andrea pushed her breast deeper into his mouth. "Oh, yes, yes, please . . . please," she gasped, her head arching backward as she embraced the pure pleasure of his touch.

She pulled away, brought his face down, enveloping him between the cushiony pillows of both breasts, rubbing, pressing, moaning at the raptures of touch, taste and feel, carrying the tactile senses to their ultimate. Finally, when she paused for breath, he pulled his head away, and brought his face down to the warm stretch of her stomach. Her voice rose higher as she cried out at the touch of his tongue that traced a fervid path downward. Her hands moved up and down his back as he reached the soft folds of her belly, caressing the deep indentation in the center, bringing his hand down to her luxurious tuft. His fingers pushed through it, feeling the thin, filamentous little strands curl around his hand. He pressed down on a Venus mound both high and soft and Andrea half screamed, her hips twisting and turning. He let his hand slide down further, pressing into the very soft flesh of full thighs held tightly together. "Oh, oh, oh, my God, my God," Andrea gasped as he pressed further until her thighs relaxed, falling open until his hand was against the damp warmth of her skin, moisture that was a herald of her fervor. His hand moved down further, the edge of her dark portal spilling out in welcome. As he touched the lubricous, velvety tip of her core, Andrea's voice burst forth in a half cry, half song.

The sound spiraled through the air, her thighs clamping closed for an instant then falling open again. She was making singsong sounds of delight and her hands clasped around his neck. He touched deeper, caressed her warm, malleable walls as Andrea's voice rose in a wild cry. "Ah, ah . . . aaaaiiieee!" she flung out, her body turning, twisting in passion. He brought himself over her, his own throbbing warmth pressing down on her jet black tuft and Andrea screamed again.

He moved, brought himself to the dark entrance, and its cluster of soft folds, and her torso lifted, offered, senses pleading and the flesh responding. He slid forward and Andrea screamed again, higher this time as her full-fleshed thighs closed around him, quivering against him as he slid forward.

"Yes, yes, oh, yes," she managed to gasp out between cries of pure pleasure and her rear lifted, fell back, lifted again, matching his smooth thrusts. Her deep breasts fell from side to side as her body convulsed, all of her completely swept up in ecstasy. She pulled his face down to her pillowy breasts and they slapped against him, her hair now a wild, flying, black crown. "More, more, more!" she cried as she responded to his deepening thrusts. Her body was flesh wreathed in ecstasy, every ample part of her tossing and twisting, writhing and crying out, and she jiggled and bounced and quaked. Her cries rose, undulating sounds in rhythm with the movements of their bodies. Suddenly, the long, singsong sounds stopped and Andrea's body fell still. But only for an instant. She stiffened, clasped herself to him, her arms, thighs, and legs enveloping him, and her head falling back as her scream exploded, rising, growing higher and higher until finally holding on a single high-pitched note. It stayed until, with a choking sound of despair, the note broke, her scream seeming to crumble away just as Fargo's own pleasure gushed.

She fell back, gasping in air, her hair draping across her face. He used one hand to brush it back and found her black eyes staring at him with a kind of disbelief. "Stay . . . stay," she murmured and he nodded, letting himself stay in her and finally her body relaxed, as if it was suddenly entirely depleted. He lay beside her, raised up on one elbow, his eyes enjoying the full-figured beauty of her. "That was quite a note you hit," he said.

"A high C, I think." She smiled, raising herself on one elbow, her deep breasts swaying gently. Her eyes grew distant as she mused aloud, "If that composer ever writes that opera about the West, I'll really be able to sing the role, thanks to you."

"Maybe it'll happen," Fargo said.*

"You'll come to hear me tonight?" Andrea said as he rose and began to dress.

"That depends on my unfinished business. I want to. I'll sure try," he said and she didn't answer, didn't move, just stayed magnificently and opulently naked before him as he finished dressing. "I have to go," he said almost apologetically.

"I'll have to make sure you'll come back," she said.

"You've already done that," he said and hurried from the room before her full-fleshed sensuousness destroyed his willpower completely.

*In fact, in 1910, the great Giacomo Puccini wrote the opera *The Girl of the Golden West (La Fanciulla del West)* about Winnie, a saloon keeper, and Dick Johnson, a cowboy, that has gone on to become a staple of the opera repertory.

4

When Fargo reached town, the morning was still young, so he decided to visit the hotel first. He squeezed the Ovaro in between a hay wagon and a Texas cotton-bed wagon across the street from the hotel, dismounting and settling down to wait. If Lola Covezza didn't appear, he had already decided he'd go inside to check further, but less than an hour had passed when luck smiled upon him. Lola came from the hotel, dressed in a dark gray blouse and dark Levi's, her long brown hair swinging loosely. She was really a petite girl, he noted as he watched her go down the street. Sidling along the building line, he stayed behind her, halting when she went into the general store.

She emerged a few minutes later carrying two bundles of yarn and a handful of knitting needles, and he watched her return to the hotel. Returning to the Ovaro, he felt relieved. She was plainly waiting, still without being contacted. She'd not be out to amuse herself knitting otherwise. But he knew that picture could change abruptly. Fargo led the Ovaro down the main street toward Doc Berenger's place. A stab of apprehension shot through him as he saw the small knot of figures outside the clinic, and Doc Berenger pushing his way through the crowd to greet him. The man's drawn, grave face made questions unnecessary. "Late last night," the doc said sadly. "In his sleep."

"He was a good man. Rest his soul," Fargo said.

"Folks are gathering on the hill. Preacher's already there. I'll be going in a few minutes," Doc Berenson said.

"Willie Whitten there?" Fargo queried.

"No. He took it real bad when he heard. Said he was going to his place, didn't want sharing memories with others. He'll be living up to his name, you can be sure."

Fargo grunted as he walked on. It wasn't hard to find the hill just west of town, a perfect burying hill, typically long with a shallow slope. He climbed to the top and joined a small group already gathered there. The service started when Doc Berenson arrived. The preacher was mercifully brief. When it ended, Fargo made his way to the bottom of the hill where he'd left the Ovaro and turned the horse south out of town. It was time to pay Whiskey Willie a visit, albeit with some misgivings. He'd have to trust whatever it was that Hank Carlson had seen in the man.

He found the shack a quarter of a mile beyond town, set back in a stand of burr oak, and when he dismounted he saw a man stumble from the shack, righting himself before coming toward him with a weaving motion. Fargo stepped forward, looking over the tall, thin man, clad in checked shirt and trousers, his black hair streaked with gray over a fine-boned face with features that were sensitive, despite the dark blood vessels that suffused it. The man paused, squinting at Fargo. "Go away, whoever you are," he grumbled, his words slurred. He turned and started to walk unsteadily back to the shack.

Fargo spied the wooden trough that was filled almost to the top with rainwater. Crossing the ground in two long strides, he grabbed Willie Whitten from behind, swung him around, lifted him into the air, and threw him into the trough. "Jesus!" Whitten roared before he hit the water and sank below its surface. He rose up and tried to climb out but Fargo pushed him under again, finally letting him up gasping and sputtering. Willie Whitten again tried to climb from the trough and again Fargo pushed him underwater and held him there. This time, when he let Willie up, the man's eyes were beginning to focus, and he showed the first signs of growing sober. Fargo pulled him from the trough and pushed him into the shack, firmly holding him with one hand. Inside the shack, Fargo saw a coffeepot resting atop a Franklin stove and Fargo pushed the man to the side as he lighted the stove.

"Take off your wet clothes," Fargo ordered.

"What the hell's all this about?" Willie Whitten demanded, his words less thick. Shivering, he began to pull off his soaked clothing. "I don't have anything worth taking, mister," he said.

"I'm not here to take anything," Fargo said, checking the coffeepot and seeing the thick liquid beginning to bubble. Whitten had his clothes off and pulled a blanket around himself as Fargo found a tin cup and filled it with coffee. "Drink," he ordered, pushing the cup into Whitten's hands. Whitten took a long draw of the strong brew and made a sour face. "Keep drinking," Fargo commanded sternly. "Finish every last damn drop of it." He waited as the man drank further, then poured another cup of coffee into him as Willie Whitten looked at him with queasiness but with clear eyes.

"Who the hell are you?" the man pushed out belligerently.

"A friend of Hank Carlson," Fargo replied.

The frown remained on Willie Whitten's face as his eyes peered at Fargo. "You're the one he called the Trailsman, aren't you . . . Skye Fargo. He told me about you," Willie said.

"Bull's-eye," Fargo said, his eyes taking in Willie Whitten's almost ascetic face. "I'm giving you a chance to do one last thing for Hank. I understand you owe him."

"That's for sure," Willie said but volunteered nothing more. Fargo didn't press the subject.

"I need your help. I need things you can do for me and maybe you can tell me things. But it'll all really be for Hank," Fargo said.

"For Hank," Whitten said, understanding and agreement in his eyes.

"I'll need you sober. No more Whiskey Willie, not till it's all over. You understand that?" Fargo said sternly.

"Until it's over," Willie agreed. "But until what's over?"

"I lost Freddie Steamer," Fargo said unhappily. "I want him back. I also want to get to the bottom of everything else that is rotten in this town."

Willie Whitten's eyes grew crafty. "What makes you think anything else is rotten?" he questioned.

"My sixth sense. I feel it, plus a few things I've come upon," Fargo answered. "But Freddie Steamer comes first."

"I heard you took care of Clay Beemis," Willie said.

"He was part of the rottenness in and about this town," Fargo said. "You get dressed in dry clothes," he said and left the shack. Fargo examined the grounds outside, saw a barn behind the shack with two horses stabled inside. Willie came out in dry clothes, eyeing the Ovaro at once.

"Mighty handsome horse," he said. "Used to raise horses. Still like them better than people."

"You know Lola Carezza? She's Freddie Steamer's girlfriend," Fargo said.

"Used to see her visit him at the jail when I was with Hank," Willie said.

"You'll watch her tonight. I'll watch until it gets dark. Then you meet me across from the hotel and take over. You see her leave with anybody, you come get me."

"Where'll you be?" Willie asked.

"At Bartley Haskell's emporium. Nothing happens, I'll come back by midnight," Fargo said.

"Got it." Willie nodded.

"See you later," Fargo said and pulled himself onto the Ovaro. He rode away with a good feeling inside him. He'd reached Willie Whitten, he felt certain. There was more to the man than a whisky-sodden town drunk. Hank had seen that. Maybe some good would come out of this for Willie Whitten when it was over. Maybe that would be Hank's legacy to his friend. He'd contribute to it if he could, Fargo told himself and rode into town, taking up his observation post across from the hotel again.

Lola emerged in midafternoon, but she was alone. She went to a dining establishment, and brought a paper bag of food back to the hotel. It was past midafternoon when he saw wagons roll into town, most of them Conestogas, some light Concord coaches, and a few three-seat platform wagons with nine-foot-long bodies and side drapes raised up to the top canopies. Every wagon was filled with young women in low-bodiced dresses, waving and calling out to the hooting onlookers as they passed. He saw the first batch of wagons pull up to Haskell's emporium. An hour later, another set of wagons, also filled with girls, came through town and rolled out of sight, plainly on their way to Emery Crater's casino. The dancing girls had arrived and it was but an hour later that dusk descended on town, and Willie Whitten appeared on a gray gelding.

He dismounted alongside Fargo, tying his horse to a post. "Afraid I wouldn't make it?" he remarked.

"Didn't even think about it," Fargo said, and saw something between pride and gratefulness touch the man's face. "You take over. Just keep watching the hotel for her. She leaves town alone or riding with somebody, come get me. Otherwise, I'll be back later."

"Good enough," Willie said and Fargo led the Ovaro off as night fell. When he reached Haskell's place, wagons were arriving in droves, buckboards, surreys, phaetons, and light pony wagons, men of all ages on their way to the emporium's wide-open doors. Fargo rubbed shoulders with four well-dressed men elbowing their way through the crowd.

"You come here often?" he asked casually.

"Often enough," one answered.

"It'll be oftener and easier now," another said. "Haskell's hiring an opera singer is a great idea. Now my wife's happy to have me come, says I'm finally getting culture."

"Same with mine," a third man added.

"The opera singer's a good excuse to get to the dancing girls," another man put in as he passed.

"You boys ever go to Emery Crater's place?" Fargo asked.

"We'll be going more now. Crater's got himself an opera singer, too. We'll be getting culture wherever we go," one of the men said as the others erupted in raucous laughter. Fargo fell back as men streamed into the auditorium. He moved to one side, a tiny furrow pressing further into his brow as he listened to the customers paying at the door. Something was out of place here. He couldn't pin down what it was, yet he felt it. When he eased himself inside along the side of the front wall, he let his gaze sweep across the entire auditorium, now almost filled with customers. Lining the walls near the stage, he saw a number of men standing quietly, each a few paces from the others, all obviously positioned as guards. Why so many? Fargo wondered. It was one more little thing that seemed out of place. He set his irritating, undefined thoughts aside for another time as the stage curtain parted and Andrea appeared, the piano and accompanist right behind her.

She wore a deep red gown, bare-shouldered that showed her ample cleavage, receiving an instant cheer from the audience. Letting his gaze roam across the audience, he saw they were almost all men, and he brought his eyes back to the stage as Andrea began to sing. He listened to the sound, beautiful and sweet and entirely lovely. The audience listened with more politeness than he'd expected, generously applauding each piece she sang. There was more applause when she finished, but he was aware that the audience had become slightly restless. After taking her bows, Andrew vanished behind the stage curtain and the audience's restlessness erupted in raucous cheers as the first set of dancing girls took the stage, all wearing scanty costumes.

This was what the audience had plainly come for, Fargo mused. The cheering and whistles went on as one group of dance girls after another took the stage, spinning and kicking, wriggling and flashing their rears and regaling their audience. When each group finished, four of the guards left the stage with them, quickly shepherding them into the back behind the curtain. The furrow dug into Fargo's brow again. It seemed a little overprotective, he thought, and finally he edged his way from the auditorium. He walked the Ovaro through the relatively quiet main street until he reached Emery Crater's casino. As at Bartley Haskell's place, wagons and tethered horses crowded around the building. He heard Ulla's voice and hurried inside to listen, finding a spot against the wall. Ulla Stenson wore a long, floor-length skirt and a sequined vest that barely contained her large breasts. An orange silk scarf was draped across her bare shoulders.

Andrea's acid comments flashed in his mind as he listened. Ulla's voice was indeed larger yet it sounded thrillingly beautiful to him, the sound more than enough to satisfy his simple demands. He'd leave the fine points to Andrea and Ulla and their obvious jealous rivalry. His eyes traveled across the crowd. They seemed a little less well-dressed than those at Haskell's, more worn boots, work clothes, and logger belts. Ulla finished her song, which turned out to be the end of her performance. She left to polite applause and, as at Haskell's, the stage immediately filled with dancing girls, kicking and shimmying in even scantier outfits. Fargo felt himself frowning again as another row of armed guards lined the back of the stage and ushered each troupe of girls away when their performance was over. It was a duplicate of things at Bartley Haskell's place and seemed just as overprotective.

Fargo watched a few moments longer and then backed out of the hall, returning to the street that was largely deserted except for the wagons and horses. He was about to collect the Ovaro when he heard a woman's voice, angered and alarmed. "No! Stop that! Get away," she said and he recognized Ulla Stenson's faint accent.

"Come on, honey. Ever do it with a cowboy?" a gruff voice said and he heard Ulla cry out.

"Stop! Let me go," she said, fear edging her voice. He threaded his way through the angled wagons, following the sound to a one-horse spring wagon at the outer perimeter of the wagons. Ulla held the reins but a burly man held the horse by the head. Suddenly he dropped his hold on the horse's cheekstrap and lunged, yanking the reins from Ulla's hands. She fell forward, practically into his arms, and he pulled her to the ground and was on top of her instantly. She tried to scream but he stuffed her orange scarf in her mouth. "Shut up," he snarled. "Never screwed an opera singer," he gloated as he started to pull Ulla's vest open.

Fargo skirted through the space between two wagons and his hand closed around the man's shoulder. "And never will, either," he said, yanking the cowboy up and flinging the man away. He glimpsed Ulla's fear-stricken face as the man pushed to his feet and came at Fargo with a bull-like charge.

"Son of a bitch!" he roared. Fargo timed his whistling uppercut as the man charged and his blow landed solidly on the man's jaw. The figure halted, quivered, then dropped to both knees. Fargo's short left hook send the man sprawling sideways, where he lay still. Stepping over the unconscious form, Fargo turned to Ulla, who fell into his arms, her large breasts pushing against his chest as her face clung tightly against his. Fargo noticed she had smooth, almost babyish skin as she clutched tightly to him, before finally pulling back.

"Thank you, thank you," she murmured and her mouth came to his, her kiss strong, commanding, her lips working softly until she pulled back. "You spend all your time doing good deeds for young ladies?" she asked, a slyness touching her eyes.

"Meaning what?" He frowned.

"It seems I recall you came to Andrea's rescue," she said, a definite impishness in her azure eyes.

"Worked out that way, just like now," he said and her arms encircled around him again.

"I'm very glad for now," she said. "Ride back with me. He might wake up and follow me."

"If you want," Fargo said. "But he won't follow. He'll be glad to have come away alive. You start. I'll get my horse." He left as she brought her arms down, then made his way to the Ovaro and joined her as she steered the wagon from the jam around the casino. Ulla led the way to a cabin much like the one in which Andrea was quartered, except on the other side of town. "Emery Crater put you up here, right?" he asked.

"That's right," she said and swung from the wagon as he dismounted. He realized he hadn't been aware of

58

how tall and statuesque she was, but she moved with both power and grace, her short blond hair swaying in rhythm with her breasts as she walked into the cabin and put a lamp on.

"Come in," she said.

"Can't. Somebody's waiting for me," Fargo said.

"Andrea Kalistro?" Ulla tossed at him impetuously.

"Now, what makes you think that?" he returned.

"You've been at her place. News travels around here."

"Just a visit," he said blandly.

"Good. Don't waste your energies with Andrea."

"Why not?"

"I'd guess she's no better at making love than she is at singing," Ulla said.

"Are sopranos always so jealous of each other?" Fargo frowned.

"Me, jealous of her? Ridiculous," Ulla said disdainfully. "I just want your time. In Sweden we believe in returning good deeds. It's a practice I'm sure you'll like."

"I'm sure I will," Fargo said.

Her arms came around him, her lips finding his again as he saw the swell of her breasts rise over the top of her vest. "I'll expect you," Ulla murmured and he smiled inwardly. She was trying to be soft and sweet but it was impossible for her not to be forward and demanding. She wasn't alone in that respect, he reminded himself. It seemed to be part of the soprano species. When she finally pulled back, he climbed onto the pinto and waved back at her. Her tall, statuesque beauty rode with him in his mind as he returned to Bearsville and the hotel, noting that the moon hadn't reached the midnight sky.

A figure opened from within the deep shadows, and Fargo recognized Willie Whitten, and swung from the saddle and came beside him. "She hasn't been out all night," Willie said.

"I'll stand watch until morning. You come back and relieve me then," Fargo said.

"I'll be here," Willie said.

"Hank ever have you do this?" Fargo asked.

"Couple of times," Willie Whitten admitted.

"Make you feel good about yourself?" Fargo ventured.

"It helped," Willie said.

"But not enough. It didn't last," Fargo commented.

Willie Whitten allowed a wry smile. "You get right down to it, don't you?" he said.

"Why not?" Fargo said and Whitten nodded. "I hope this time it lasts longer," Fargo added.

The man thought for a moment. "It just might," he said.

"Why's that?" Fargo asked.

"Hank was always helping me and I was grateful to him for that. But he was always doing me a good deed. You're not doing that. You're taking a chance on me. That puts a different light on things, makes a man feel different about himself."

"Let's hope so," Fargo said and Willie Whitten smiled as he hurried away. Fargo had the feeling it was his first smile in a long, long time. Settling down, Fargo surveyed the dark, silent street. There was little activity as the night drew on and Lola didn't leave the hotel. Morning finally came, and the street started to take on movement. Willie Whitten appeared, coming from around the corner of the building next to where

Fargo waited. A hard glance at the man revealed to Fargo no signs of liquor, his eyes clear, his step firm.

"I'll take over," Willie said.

"She stayed in for the night," Fargo said.

"Get some shut-eye. Where'll I find you if something happens?"

"Take the road south from town. There's a cluster of blue beech trees set back from the road. I'll bed down there," Fargo said.

"I know the spot. Come back when you're ready," Willie said as Fargo led the Ovaro away, taking to the saddle when he was a dozen yards away. Wagons and horsemen were already filling the town when he spotted Andrea and Ulla, both climbing into their respective rigs, hitched almost alongside each other. Ulla saw him first, and called out. He saw Andrea turn, a possessive little smile instantly lighting across her lips.

" 'Morning, ladies." Fargo greeted them. "Don't tell me you two are together."

"Hardly," Ulla replied. "I came in early to do a little shopping."

"I needed a few things at the general store as well," Andrea said. "Where are you going?" she asked.

"He's going to visit me," Ulla said.

"Why would he do that?" Andrea asked.

"Maybe he'd like to hear some good singing for a change," Ulla said.

"Then he'll most certainly be visiting me," Andrea snapped.

"Sorry, girls," Fargo cut in, "I'm not out to visit either of you. Got some other business to do." He decided not to say he intended to get some sleep. That would only bring on more invitations, he knew. "I'll find another time to come visit," he said and moved the Ovaro on.

"I'll be waiting," Ulla called.

"I'll be remembering," Andrea said pointedly and Fargo saw Ulla frown at her as she climbed into her rig. Fargo urged the Ovaro into a canter, rode into the stand of blue beech, and bedded down. But despite his weariness, sleep refused to come right away. Instead, the evening before nagged at his mind and he found himself thinking about the incidents that caused his brow to furrow so often. He couldn't pin down any answers but he did manage to define the things that gnawed at him, bothersome, disturbing pieces of a puzzle that refused to fit. He never liked things that didn't add up. They hung in the air like unfinished sentences, leaving their real meaning unsaid. But when sleep finally came he had at least isolated the questions, and slept with that much satisfaction, small as it was.

It was almost midafternoon when he woke, annoyed at himself for having slept so long. After refreshing himself at a stream, he returned to town and joined Willie Whitten across from the hotel. "Sorry. Meant to be here earlier," he said.

"Nothing much happened anyway. She went to the bakery and then came right back," Willie said.

"Got some questions that have been bothering me. Maybe you've got a take on them," Fargo said. "For one, I can't figure why Haskell has so many guards shepherding the dance girls. Saw the same thing at Emery Crater's place."

"Hank used to wonder about that, too. Never could come up with an answer but it always bothered him."

"Another thing that bothers me about both

Haskell's and Crater's. They're both paying good money for their opera stars. Andrea told me as much. Then they're paying their dance girls, their help, cleaning boys, attendants, and all those guards. But there's not much drinking at their establishments. Their only real take is the admission price. That can't be bringing in enough money. It just doesn't add up," Fargo said.

"Hank could never understand that, either," Willie said.

"Also, I still don't understand why they don't put their opera stars in one of the rooms, same as they do with the dance girls. Why put them out in a cabin all alone?" Fargo frowned.

"Don't have an answer for that one, either. Maybe the singers wanted a place to practice," Willie suggested.

"They could do that better in the auditorium. There's a piano in both places. There's nothing in the cabins," Fargo said. "There are a lot of strange things going on that just don't fit right."

"Hank always said that about the Haskell and Crater operations but he could never get a chance to prove anything more," Willie said. "Maybe there isn't anything more."

"Maybe there is. I get a real funny feeling from it," Fargo said and Willie shrugged. Willie, too, was not easy to fathom, Fargo decided. Without the whiskey holding him in its grip, he seemed both intelligent and quietly sensitive. "How did Hank become a special friend to you, Willie?" he asked.

Willie offered a small, almost winsome smile, his lips pursing as he thought for a moment. "I guess you could say he was the only one who understood weakness," Willie Whitten said.

It was Fargo's turn to smile. "That doesn't tell me a lot," he said.

"I had a kid brother who was killed in an accident I should've been there to prevent. I started to hit the bottle then. Hank was the only one in town who didn't condemn me, write me off, or look down at me. He understood that not all of us are strong."

"You see yourself as weak?" Fargo probed.

"What else? The strong can get over guilt. The strong pick up the pieces and go on. The weak hide from themselves, each in their own way. I picked the bottle," Willie said.

"Maybe that's not weakness at all. Maybe you're only seeing it that way," Fargo said.

"What would you call it?"

"It's an emotion so strong it won't let go. It's caring for something so strong it overwhelms, paralyzes. Then it's a strength that works in reverse, a strength turned back on itself. But it's still strength, not weakness. Trick is, you have to turn that strength back into something positive. I think that's what Hank wanted you to find a way to do," Fargo said.

"You give it words he never did," Willie said thoughtfully. "I'll be thanking you for that." He started to leave when Fargo's sudden whisper stopped him. Two figures had halted in front of the hotel and were tethering their horses. They looked around furtively, nervously.

"This might be what I've been waiting for," Fargo said as the two men hurried into the hotel. Willie waited beside him, and not more than a few minutes passed when Lola Carezza came out with both men. One took her onto his horse with him and both started down the wide main street of town. "Time for trailing," Fargo said.

"I can go with you," Willie said.

"I don't know what I'll run into. When did you last use a six-gun?" Fargo asked. "You think you're steady enough to use one now?" There was no answer, and Fargo patted Willie's shoulder. "Stay here and wait for me. There may be a lot more to do. In fact, there's something to do now. I want you to look in on both Andrea and Ulla, keep an eye on them."

"All right," Willie said.

"You can tell them I told you to do it," Fargo said. "I'll check in with you at your place when I get back."

Willie gave him a sidelong glance. "How do you figure to get Freddie Steamer all on your own now that he has his gang with him again?"

"Haven't figured that out yet," Fargo said as he swung onto the Ovaro and rode from town. He hung back as the three riders lit out, continuing to stay back and following their tracks. Willie's question clung to him. He had to find a way to get Freddie Steamer, who now had his gang with him again, plus Lola. Lola wasn't of any real importance to Freddie Steamer, except for whatever practical help or pleasure she could furnish. Steamer didn't seem like the kind for emotional attachments. But neither was Lola, Fargo was certain, and he found himself thinking more about the young woman. Lola Carezza had waited patiently while Steamer was in jail and had tried to help him escape. But he had seen and known too many Lola Carezzas over the years. She was clearly not the faithful, pining, loving type.

Lola had waited for Freddie because she was committed to the money he had salted away. Perhaps he'd even promised her a piece of it. She could be more important than Fargo had anticipated and he thought further about it, polishing the plans that had taken form in his mind. As the day drew to a close, he had made his final preparations, and rode closer to where he could listen to the path of the two horses. They went on until the forest night veiled the world in darkness. When he heard them come to a halt, Fargo reined up the Ovaro, swung to the ground, and crept forward on foot, his horse following quietly behind. He heard the sound of their voices and halted, listening as they bedded down. Silence rested over the forest and finally, the moon filtered its way through the heavy overhang of leaves and branches, providing scant light.

Fargo crouched, silent as a salamander on a rock, letting enough time go by before moving forward, one careful step after another until the moonlight let him see the three figures asleep in a half circle, Lola lying apart from the two men. He hung the Ovaro's reins over a low branch and crept forward alone, moving past the two men and halting beside Lola. Bending low over her, Fargo brought his fist down in a short, sharp blow that just clipped the point of her jaw.

Her body went entirely limp, her head lolling over to one side. "Sorry," he murmured as he lifted her and slung her over his shoulder. Carrying her, he slipped away from the two sleeping men and on soft, careful steps, brought her to the Ovaro. He laid her facedown over the saddle and walked the horse until he was far enough away to slide into the saddle along with her. He rode through the night and didn't stop till Lola stirred and woke. He halted, lifting her to sit in the saddle as she took a moment to focus on him.

"Jesus, it's you!" she said. "You crazy?"

"Not the last time I looked," Fargo said. "But I do aim to get Freddie Steamer."

"Hell, you can't get him all by yourself. You *are* crazy," Lola sneered. "You won't even get away with this. They'll come after you when they wake up."

"I'm counting on that. As for Freddie, I'll get him. But whether I do or not, you won't be getting any of that money he robbed and stashed away," Fargo said. "Not unless you help me, that is," he added, letting Lola frown at him.

"Me help you. That's a laugh," she snapped.

"Only you won't be laughing," Fargo said, leaning close to let her see the icy blue of his eyes. He watched her glare back and then saw the discomfort come into her eyes. "Let me explain something to you, girl. Your boyfriend killed a lot of innocent people during his bank robbing. I don't much care what happens to anyone who throws in with him. That includes you, honey. You can choose to live or die and I don't give a damn which it is. That means you can help me or not. It's your call. Help me, and you'll get to see a piece of the money Freddie has. Don't help me, and you'll never see a thin dime."

"You're bullshitting me. How are you going to get me any of that money?" she tossed at him.

"I've the right to reward anybody who helps me get Freddie. Ten percent is the standard amount. It's yours if you help me bring him in," he said and she continued to stare at him as her thoughts raced. "Believe me, it's the only way you'll see any of that money. You don't think Freddie's really going to give you any of it, do you?"

"He said he would," she returned.

67

Fargo let out a harsh laugh. "All Freddie's going to do is screw you, in every way," he said. "You know that deep down inside. You're just hoping he hands you a little bit of it, or that you can steal some and take off. I'm offering you a guaranteed ten percent."

Her eyes narrowed at him. "How do I know *you* won't screw me?"

"You've been around. You can read men. You know I'll keep my word," he said. "About everything," he added pointedly and knew she understood.

"If I say no, what then?" Lola asked.

"I've a nice cave waiting for you. It can be a safe, temporary place for you or it can be your tomb. That's your call, too," Fargo said nonchalantly and watched the whirling thoughts behind her eyes. "I don't have a lot of time or patience," he said as she glowered.

"I don't really know much," she said finally, and he knew the answer for what it was. He had won.

"Let's start with what you do know. Where were they taking you?" he questioned.

"North, past Black Swan Lake," Lola said.

"Is that where Freddie is?" he asked and she nodded. "And the rest of them?" She nodded again. "How many are there besides Freddie?"

"Five," she said.

"Including the two who came for you?"

"Yes," Lola confirmed. Plans quickly took shape in Fargo's mind.

"They'll come looking for you, of course. We're going to give them a trail to follow, only they won't find you at the end of it," he said, then stepped forward and abruptly tore a piece from the sleeve of her blouse. He dropped it on the ground, then climbed onto the Ovaro, pulling her up in front of him. Though a petite girl, Lola was very soft and round, he felt as she sat back against him. He rode on for another thousand yards or so and halted. "Drop one of your sandals," he said. She slipped the sandal off, letting it fall to the ground, and they went on again. He picked soft places in the ground that would show hoofprints and when he halted again he was at the edge of a heavy stand of black oak. "You have a comb?" he asked and Lola took a short tortoiseshell comb from her pocket. He took it, threw it on the ground, and turned the Ovaro into the deep forest.

He rode carefully, now, skirting shrubs and low branches, riding until the trees thinned. They soon emerged at a row of high rocks and caves. He chose the first cave and pulled Lola from the horse.

"What's this for? I told you what you wanted to know," she flared.

"This is just so you don't get a change of heart," Fargo said as he bound her ankles, then her wrists.

"Goddamn better be," Lola swore as he fastened her securely to a tall sliver of rock at one side of the cave. "What if you don't get back?" she asked, a note of fear trembling on the edge of her resentment.

"Then we're both in a lot of trouble," he said. She was still muttering after him as he left her. She'd be able to work herself free in a few days, Fargo felt certain, and turned his thoughts to the things he had to do. He stayed in heavy tree cover as he rode. The two men would start searching for Lola as soon as they woke and when Fargo reached the spot where he'd left the last of the markers, Lola's comb, he settled down in the trees to wait. He knew it'd take them a while to stumble onto the first marker, so he leaned back against the dark bark of the oak and catnapped. It turned out to take them twice as long as Fargo had expected, as the day was sliding toward an end when he finally heard the sound of the horses. He rose at once, and moved to the edge of the tree line, where he watched the two men find Lola's comb.

"Here, look," one of the men called out. He was the shorter of the two, with a thick black mustache on a broad face.

"You think she dropped it on purpose for us to find?" the other questioned.

"Maybe, but we know for sure they came this way, she and whoever the hell took her," the other one said.

"I still think we ought to go and tell Freddie," the second man said.

"And lose their trail altogether?" the mustached one answered. "Heck no. Let's keep on." He was peering at the hoof marks in the soil when Fargo interrupted.

"The trail's over, gents," Fargo said and both men looked at the trees with shock flooding their faces. "Drop your guns, real slow," Fargo ordered as he stepped forward. The two men just stared at him and Fargo saw their eyes go to his hand, resting on the butt of the Colt. He saw the thought forming in their eyes at once and sized both up for what they were—small-time thugs filled with stupid arrogance, men who always thought they were better than they were. Fargo saw the conclusions forming in their eyes: his gun wasn't out, and he'd hold no advantage over them once they got their hands on their guns.

"Easy, mister, whatever you say." The mustached one slyly grinned.

Fargo sighed. "Don't do anything dumb," he said almost wearily. But his eyes were on their hands and he saw what most men would have missed; the almost imperceptible tightening of their fingers as they touched their guns. Fargo drew the Colt with the speed of forked lightning, the revolver up and firing while both men were still yanking their guns out. The shots struck home as the two men dropped from their horses in unison, hitting the ground at the same time. One lay still. The other stirred, but only for a moment, and Fargo stepped to their silent forms. "I said don't do anything dumb," he muttered, knowing he'd receive no answer. He turned away, climbed onto the Ovaro, and turned the horse north. He rode at a good pace without pushing his mount, aware that he was racing the day as it steadily dwindled.

But there was still light when he arrived at Black Willow lake, and he skirted one shore, slowing but keeping north. When the dusk deepened he slowed further, putting the horse to a walk as night fell. When it was too dark to pick out the way, Fargo finally slid from the saddle and led the way on foot. Another half hour had passed when he came to a sudden halt, seeing a pinpoint of light shine through the trees. Shifting direction, Fargo moved forward, closing in on the light which grew larger, emanating from inside a ramshackle house set in a small clearing. Fargo dropped the Ovaro's reins to the ground and crept closer alone, seeing a house with its rear half almost collapsed in on itself, made of loose boards with a caved-in roof. The front part of the house seemed intact and Fargo crouched, then moved across the cleared land to where lamplight shone from an open doorway and a window without glass.

Staying low, Fargo halted against the front wall of the house, just beneath the window a few feet from the open doorway. Carefully, he raised his head enough to peer over the edge of the windowsill. Four men were inside the nearly barren room, one of them Freddie Steamer, his manner agitated as he made short, pacing movements along one wall. "Somethin' wrong," Freddie Steamer rasped. "They should've been here long before now, goddamn it."

"Like what?" one of the others asked.

"How the hell do I know? That bastard Fargo's out there on the loose someplace. That's enough for me. But somethin's wrong. I'm damn sure of that," Steamer said.

"You want us to go out look for her and Zeke and Charlie?" another asked.

Steamer hesitated, but only for a moment. "No, goddammit. They got their asses in a sling, they can stay there. They're not gonna drag us into it. We're getting out of here," he said and Fargo saw him reach for a jacket. Dropping down, Fargo ran in a crouch and once he reached the trees, whirled to see Steamer and the other three men hurry from the house. As he watched, they went to the collapsed rear of the house, and began to pull aside boards and fallen pieces of roof. While Steamer and two of the men tore at the boards, the third man went behind the house and reappeared leading a brown gelding with a white blaze on its forehead. Freddie Steamer was the first to emerge from the rear of the house and Fargo saw he carried a large, canvas sack. The others followed, each carrying similar sacks, which Fargo soon recognized as bank money bags.

The others returned to the rubble at the rear of the house, pulling out more sacks as Steamer began to load each bag onto the horse. Finally, the last sack was brought out and tied onto one of the horses, now the packhorse. When he finished, Steamer slung a large horse blanket over the sacks and turned toward the others. "Get the horses. I want distance between us and this place before sunup," Steamer said. One of the men hurried to the back of the house, and returned leading the horses.

"What about Sam and Charley?" he asked.

"No show, no split," Steamer said, frowning at the three men. "Since when do you mind splitting money four ways instead of six?" he pushed at them. They glanced at each other, shrugged, then started to climb on their horses. Steamer took the lead, the packhorse beside him, and led the way from the ramshackle hideaway.

Fargo felt for the Colt, but he left the gun in its holster. He had to stop them, somehow. But it wouldn't be easy. These were men in the last stages of a haphazard plot, suddenly afraid and uneasy, but determined to finally get away with everything they had stolen. They would react to any attack with desperate ferocity. They'd fight to the very end, having everything to lose. He knew he had to find some way to give himself a chance, and he watched them ride off with serious misgivings.

5

He returned to the Ovaro, climbed onto the horse, and began to follow. He hung back far enough not to be heard, yet close enough to glimpse the four riders as they moved single file through the sparse moonlight that filtered into the forest. Freddie Steamer led the others, the packhorse alongside him. Fargo cursed softly. They were too spread out—he could easily bring down at least one but the others would react and scatter instantly. He needed something more than a moment's surprise. He needed them disconcerted so he could get the most out of the instant before the element of surprise was gone. He needed a diversion, their attention focused on something else.

Moving carefully, Fargo kept ahold of his patience, part of any trailsman's stealthy weaponry, perhaps the one thing that separated the real tracker from the amateur, the hunter from the follower. The moon had risen into the midnight sky when Fargo heard the sounds from ahead change in character, and he drew the pinto to a quick halt. Listening, he let his ears become his eyes. The men up ahead were talking in short, terse sentences and Fargo's ears caught the soft sound of bedrolls being dropped onto the ground. They were preparing to bed down and get some sleep before going on come morning. Fargo swung from the saddle, resting on one knee until there were only the night sounds of buzzing, clacking insects. He waited more before he rose, dropped the Ovaro's reins over a branch, and went forward alone.

Peering through the trees, he found the four men fast asleep on the ground. Though they lay with two much room between them, they'd tethered their horses together on low branches, the packhorse at the edge of the other four. Moving forward on steps silent as a cougar on the prowl, Fargo edged to the packhorse and carefully unwound its reins from a branch. He backed the horse a few steps, and heard one of the men turn and grunt in his sleep. Fargo held the horse in place with one hand against its neck, soothing the skittish animal. The figure fell back to sleep as Fargo drew one hand back, then brought his palm down with all his strength on the horse's rump in a stinging slap. The horse let out a whinny of protest as it bolted, launching into an instant gallop as it streaked through the trees.

Freddie Steamer and his men sprang awake instantly, shouting curses as they caught a glimpse of the horse sprinting away. Fargo had already dropped flat on his stomach in the underbrush, and watched as the four men ran to their horses, leaping into their saddles and racing after the fleeing packhorse. They'd wonder about how he came to bolt later. Right now, all their concentration was on catching the horse with all their stolen loot on it. They didn't bother to throw a glance right or left as they started off after the escaping packhorse. Fargo took aim at the nearest two riders, and fired in quick succession. Both men flew from their horses as if they'd been pulled off by a single lariat.

"Goddamn!" he heard Freddie Steamer curse, and swinging the Colt toward his voice, Fargo saw the man had already flung himself out of the saddle, diving into the brush. The other man had done the same, Fargo saw as he caught a glimpse of his diving figure. Fargo scooted backward on his stomach, deeper into the trees where he rose to rest against the warty, gray bark of a hackberry. He heard Freddie Steamer move, flattening himself against a broad tree trunk. "That's got to be you, Fargo," the man called. "You son of a bitch." Fargo didn't answer. He had reduced the odds by fifty percent. He wasn't about to dilute them by disclosing his location to a bullet. Steamer called out again. "Not this time, you bastard!" he shouted. "You're a dead man, Fargo." Fargo heard him crawling away from the tree, moving back further into the forest. He then caught a glimpse of a second dark figure as it darted through trees.

It was the other man, who was meeting Steamer. Fargo heard their whispered exchanges and then there was only silence. Fargo inclined his head, his ears straining to pick up any sound. But there was none. Both men remained mute, their strategy agreed upon. Under other circumstances, Fargo might have smiled, he realized. But not now. Freddie Steamer had already shown that he could do the unexpected. And he was doing it again. First, he was trying to outfox his foe. Steamer hoped their silence would make Fargo think they were crawling away. Silence would make him come after them, Steamer hoped. Or he hoped his foe would become alarmed, and grow tired of waiting or simply lose patience and come searching.

Fargo's lips now allowed a wry smile. He knew the two men were not crawling away. These were no

Shoshone warriors who could crawl through the forest silent as a blacksnake. He'd have heard their clumsy efforts. No, Steamer had decided to stay. If he couldn't lure his foe into making a mistake, he'd wait for something else—the light of morning. Fargo's mouth hardened. Day would give the two bandits a distinct advantage. They could see him as quickly as he could them, and have two guns ready to fire. It had suddenly become a waiting game. Fargo leaned against the tree and began to form his own plan. Trying to crawl forward, to move in on Steamer, was out of the question. Even he couldn't be silent enough, Fargo realized. The night was too still, the leaves too dry and too loose on the forest floor. Somewhere along the way, they'd send their rustling alarm echoing to Steamer's ears.

But he'd not sit by until morning. He'd not let day become their ally. His eyes swept the moonlit forest as he turned plans over in his mind. Finally, he quietly rose and stretched his arms upward, grasping the thickest of the low branches over his head. Using all his muscular discipline, he kept his body stiffened, not letting it swing and brush against the tree trunk as he lifted himself. When he was able to pull one leg over the branch, he lay still for a moment, regaining his breath until he could silently shift to a better position on the branch. He lay there, his gaze moving over the forest floor below, but the weak moonlight revealed nothing. He had to climb higher, he knew, and as he peered upward, he saw two thinner branches that could bring him to a thicker one, which would serve as a good perch.

But thin branches could creak and rustle their leaves. Steamer and his man would surely hear the sound and all his plans would shatter in a hail of gun-

77

fire. He decided to lie still and wait for the reliability of nature, taking a firmer grip of the branch and letting his body relax. Time moved with maddening slowness but finally the night's silence was suddenly broken as the baying call of distant wolves filled the air. They raised their voices as they called to each other, one lobo answering another. Fargo pushed himself up on the branch, hurrying to use the cover of the baying calls to mask the sound of his own movements. He reached up, pulled himself onto the next branch, and felt it creak and the foliage dip, leaves moving against each other. He continued climbing onto the next thin branch, which also dipped and rustled its leaves. He never thought he'd be so glad to hear the sound of timberwolves, Fargo realized, as he reached the next thick branch. He settled himself into the crook of the branch, positioning himself just as the baying ebbed and the forest fell silent again.

He glanced around at his perch on the hackberry, and made a mental note that another branch jutted out halfway around to the rear of the tree. Leaning back, he settled down and waited as the moon made its way to the far edge of the sky, its pale light fading away entirely to plunge the forest into almost total darkness. He flexed his leg muscles to prevent their cramping up in the awkwardness of his position. Finally the first tentative touch of gray sifted through the trees. Slowly, the forest took shape again, branches, leaves, and trees standing out against the curtain of darkness. Fargo drew the Colt and leaned forward on the crook of the branch, letting his gaze travel across the forest floor.

The day was beginning to flood through the forest when he caught movement below, only a few yards beyond the tree where he perched. It was Freddie

Steamer, six-gun in hand, motioning with one arm to the second figure that soon appeared. At Steamer's signal, the second man started to cautiously come forward. Certain their quarry was hunkered down somewhere in front of them, they came in from opposite sides to lay down a deadly cross fire. Their plan would probably have worked had Fargo stayed on the ground, he saw as he leaned forward on the branch. Heavy foliage obscured Freddie Steamer, so Fargo's eyes went to the other man who came into sight. Fargo raised the Colt, adjusted his balance on the branch, and fired a single shot. The man, who was bent over in a crouch as he moved forward, suddenly arched backward as the bullet struck, landing in a thick bush where only his motionless legs protruded.

Freddie Steamer whirled, his eyes lifting to the tree as Fargo expected. He fired off a blast of bullets as he cursed in rage and Fargo felt the shots slam into the tree around him as Steamer kept up his furious barrage. Reaching back, Fargo took hold of an adjoining branch and swung himself around to the rear of the tree as a bullet tore through his shirt. He heard Steamer curse as his gun clicked, empty. Fargo knew the man would need a dozen seconds to reload as he slid down the rear of the tree, ignoring the pain as branches clawed at him. Dropping hard to the ground, he sprawled forward, rolling and coming up in a crouch behind another tree.

Steamer would be crouched waiting to let loose another barrage of shots, Fargo thought. But once again, Steamer had done the unexpected. Certain that at least one of the hail of bullets had hit their mark, the thought reinforced by the sound of Fargo falling from the tree, Freddie Steamer was now running, crashing through brush. But not to hide, or to find a better spot to fire from, Fargo realized, and he rose to his feet, whirling to run back to where he'd left the Ovaro. Reaching the horse, Fargo vaulted into the saddle, having to use another few precious seconds to turn the pinto around. Fargo was certain Freddie Steamer had reached his horse by now, but a knowing smile came to his lips. He suddenly had another ally, and its name was greed. Steamer couldn't just flee. He couldn't ride away from the one thing he'd robbed and killed to have, the one thing around which he'd built his miserable life. It was impossible. He could no more run away from the money than he could run from himself.

Fargo sent the Ovaro forward, but not in a frenzied chase. He rode carefully, his ears straining for the sounds from ahead of him. Finally he heard what he listened for—the beat of horse's hooves. He shifted direction and put the pinto into a gallop. When he finally caught sight of Freddie Steamer racing through the thick of the forest, a satisfied grunt escaped him. He had been so very right. Freddie Steamer now fled, but laboriously pulling the packhorse behind him. It was slowing him down some, of course, but Steamer hoped his barrage of bullets had prevented him from being chased. Still, he was taking chances, Fargo saw, racing through the dense trees, risking a collision if his horse made a misstep. The Ovaro's powerful hindquarters skirted through narrow gaps in the trees and he quickly closed in on the fleeing rider. As he neared, Steamer heard the sound of another horse and Fargo enjoyed the surprised look on the man's face as he turned to look back.

Swerving, Fargo sent the Ovaro racing forward through the heavy tree cover to draw abreast of

Steamer. But Steamer flung himself down in the saddle, and as he sped past tree after tree he presented only a small, split-second target. Fargo swore, aware that he had only three bullets in his Colt and only one other round in his gun belt. Staying abreast of Steamer, Fargo's eyes shifted to where Steamer's reins stretched in a straight, taut line to the packhorse. Where the reins joined the rein chains they knotted, grew wider and thicker, but stayed stretched out. Fargo maneuvered the pinto closer and took careful aim, brought his body into perfect synchronization with his horse's steady gait, and fired two shots. The knotted section of the reins blew apart and the packhorse immediately slowed. Fargo saw Freddie Steamer spin in the saddle, alarm and astonishment flooding his face as he saw himself holding the limp reins.

"Goddamn!" he cursed and did exactly what Fargo was certain he'd do. He yanked his horse to a halt, turned, and came racing back for the packhorse, his reaction automatic. As he charged back, he became an open target. Fargo came out of the trees, willing to give the man a last chance.

"Drop the gun. It's over," he called.

But Freddie Steamer, his face twisted with fury, a man past thinking or reasoning, a man acting only out of the greed that held his heart in its unyielding grip, raised his gun to shoot. He never had a chance. The Colt barked and Freddie Steamer shuddered in the saddle for a moment before toppling from the horse. He fell slowly, a terrible finality to his movements, and lay still. Fargo waited for a moment, then urged the pinto forward as he holstered the Colt. Freddie Steamer's final moments had been marked for him long ago. He had simply chosen a different path to the same end.

Fargo took hold of the packhorse, tied the frayed reins to the Ovaro's saddle horn, and began the long ride back through the forest. He kept a steady pace during the long trek and day still illuminated the land when he finally reached the rows of rocks and caves. Dismounting, he pulled the horses into the first cave and saw Lola's head lift as he entered. "Dammit, it's time you came back," she spat at him. He untied her and she quickly rubbed circulation back into her wrists and pushed to her feet.

"You don't look any worse for wear," he said as he took in the bold thrust of her hips, the annoyed push of her modest breasts against the fabric of her top.

"What happened to Freddie? Where is he?" Lola questioned.

"He decided against a hangman's noose," Fargo said. Her expression didn't change as her eyes went to the bank sacks.

"You going to count it all?" she asked.

"No. There's a bank in Bearsville. They'll count it and hold it until the other banks send someone for their money. You helped me. You'll get the ten percent I promised you," Fargo said. Lola took in his words with a mask over her eyes. She could be a good poker player, he decided. "Let's ride," he said and turned to the pinto, starting to pull himself into the saddle. Lola could also move with speed and deftness, he found out as he felt the Colt yanked from his holster. His hand flew back to grab the gun but he was too late. Whirling, he stepped back to the ground to see the Colt pointed between his eyes. He also noted that Lola's hand held the gun with unwavering steadiness.

"Put it down, girl," Fargo said. "You can't do this."

"Hell I can't," Lola tossed back calmly.

"It won't work for you. You're not thinking right," he said.

"I'm thinking fine," she said. "I'm thinking ten percent's not enough. A hundred percent's much better."

Fargo's thoughts raced. Lola was a product of her world, a place where hardness and selfishness ruled. But she was smart, in her own venal, self-centered way. He had to try to reach her good senses before she pulled the trigger. He had no illusions she'd balk at the task. "Listen to me. You've a chance to get a lot of money. You'll have it free and clear. You can make a new life for yourself, and a very good one," he said.

"But a much better one with *all* the money," Lola said.

"No, not a better one," he said, desperately marshaling arguments, trying to find a way to reach her. "You'll be running again, always looking over your shoulder. They'll come looking for me. They'll put two and two together and come up with you."

"They might never find you in here. It could be months before they do," Lola said with a practical logic he couldn't refute. "I'll be long gone by then. There are a lot of places in this world where they'll never find me."

Fargo swore under his breath. He wasn't reaching her. She was too hardened by her yesterdays, too much an echo of Freddie Steamer. She had her own brand of selfish logic that was past changing. He eyed the Colt. It hadn't moved an inch. He had one avenue left. There was one other part of her that was as built-in as her hard-bitten self-protectiveness. It was there in the way she had looked at him, in the thrust of her hips, in the simmering quality she exuded. Lola's own brand of sensuousness was always there, always waiting, always ready to turn on or be turned on.

He drew a deep breath. "You win, honey," he said and saw surprise come into her eyes. He looked at the bank sacks and back to her. "I'm the one who's a fool, been one too long. How about a partner?"

"You're kidding," she said warily.

"No, I've been working for too little, for too long. I want more. You'll need somebody to help you get away with all that money. You'll never make it alone. You know what the world's like out there," Fargo said. Lola stared at him but he saw her turning his words in her mind. "You need someone. It might as well be me," he added.

Her eyes narrowed at him. "How do I know you'll stick with me?" she asked. The question let him smile silently. He had reached her, after all.

"You asked and answered that one before. You know I'm the kind who keeps his word," he said and saw the new light slide into her eyes. "Partners, Lola? We can pull it off together. We can do a lot of things together, too, things you'll enjoy as much as the money," he seductively pressed.

Her eyes stayed narrowed, but he saw the thoughts whirling behind them. And he saw something else he waited for. The Colt dipped, an automatic reaction as she relaxed. It was that moment he wanted. His hands shot out, slamming into hers, his fingers closing around the Colt. The gun went off as her finger tightened on the trigger, and he felt the hot blast of it against his cheek.

"Son of a bitch!" Lola screamed. But he yanked upward, and tore the gun from her hand as it went off again.

"Goddamn you," Lola shouted as she tried to claw his face. He got one shoulder up, avoided her raking nails, spun her around, and flung her into the wall. She hit hard, bounced and fell to the ground. He had her up before she could regain her feet, spun her again, and scooped up the rope with which he had originally tied her. Wrapping it around both her wrists, he knotted it as she tried to kick him. He spun her again and bound her arms to her sides. She spat vehement curses at him along with her furious glare. "Bastard! Rotten bastard. Your word's no damn good," she swore.

"I never gave it, honey," Fargo said. "You should've learned from Freddie. Crime doesn't pay. Neither does greed." He pulled her with him, hoisted her onto the Ovaro, and climbed on behind her. With the packhorse in tow, he rode from the cave as night fell. Setting a steady pace, he rode through the night, stopping only to let the horses rest. It was morning when he reached Bearsville, and they astonished the banker and his clerk as they were opening the bank. Fargo told them what had happened as they carried the sacks into the bank, locking them in the safe as he tied Lola to the hitching post. He arranged with the two bankers to have them contact the other banks so they'd send representatives to claim their stolen money.

He went outside to Lola, untied her from the hitching post, and led her to the sheriff's office, then deposited her in what had been Freddie Steamer's cell. "I'll be sending someone to see to you," he said.

Lola's eyes shot daggers at him. "I helped you. I told you where to find Freddie. You've no cause to hold me," she accused.

"You tried to kill me for the money. I'd call that pretty good cause," Fargo said.

"Damn you to hell," she shouted as he locked the cell and went into the outer office. He rummaged through a drawer in the desk, found what he sought after, and hurried outside to the Ovaro. Riding down the street, he passed Bartley Haskell's emporium and noted that almost all the second-floor windows were closed, the curtains drawn. He carried a small frown with him as he rode on from town, turning south and eventually arriving at Willie Whitten's shack. Willie came out as Fargo rode up and dismounted, seeing Fargo's penetrating glance hold on him.

Willie offered a wry smile. "Looking for Whiskey Willie?" he said.

"Wouldn't say that," Fargo said. "But I wondered, I'll admit."

"Can't blame you for that," Willie said.

"I'm real pleased," Fargo said and Willie's smile widened.

"You get Freddie Steamer?" he asked and Fargo told him what had happened. "Can't say I'm surprised. Bad pennies stay bad."

"What's been going on here? You keep tabs on Andrea and Ulla?" Fargo queried.

"Yep. Andrea's been getting madder every hour you haven't shown," Willie said.

"No surprise there. And Ulla?"

"She's asked, too, but not as heated up about it," Willie said.

"Get your horse. I want you to see to Lola. She's a prisoner until I decide what to do about her," Fargo said. He took a shiny object from his pocket and pinned it on Willie's shirt. "Deputy Whitten," he proclaimed. "This town needs a deputy sheriff. You'll be it until Hank's replacement gets here. He can do his own choosing then."

Willie ran a finger over the badge. "A lot of folks are going to be surprised, especially when I arrest them for being drunk and disorderly," Willie said.

"It's your job now. Do it right and surprise will turn to respect," Fargo said as Willie rode out beside him. He reined up halfway to town. "I'll stop by at Andrea's cabin. You go on, get Lola some food. I know she's hungry as hell by now," Fargo said. "You'll find some extra guns and holsters in the outer office. Strap one on." Willie nodded and Fargo turned from the road, riding into the woods and finally drawing up at Andrea's cabin.

She came out at once, and fastened him with an imperious stare. "You didn't say you'd be gone this long," she snapped.

"Didn't know how long myself," he said.

"I kept looking for you," Andrea said.

"Looking where?" he asked blandly.

"Different places," she said evasively as he smiled. She let go of her imperiousness and came to him, her arms encircling his neck. "Thanks for sending your deputy to look in on me," Andrea murmured. Fargo smiled inwardly: Willie had been diplomatic, letting each of them think she was the only one he'd been sent to check on. He made a note to thank Willie as Andrea's full lips met his mouth.

"You singing tonight?" he asked when she pulled back.

"No, not till the weekend," she answered.

"How come?" he queried.

"Most of the dancing girls left yesterday. Some trouble with Mr. Haskell," Andrea said, staying pressed against him.

"What kind of trouble?" Fargo asked.

"I don't know. I don't ask and I don't care. I'm just here to sing," she said.

A frown crossed his brow.

"*I* care, and I want to ask," Fargo said.

She gave him a slightly pained look. "I don't know why," she sniffed.

"Well I'm going to find out," Fargo said.

"You'll be back?" she said.

"Hope so," Fargo said.

"Make it so," she said loftily. He kissed her cheek and swung onto the pinto, then rode away, hurrying down the road to town. Andrea's news stayed with him, disturbing him though he wasn't at all sure why. But he knew that inside himself a knot of strange, unexplained things was gathering like storm clouds. Her words had explained only one thing—the curtained windows on the second floor of Haskell's place—and as he reached the emporium he drew to a halt and dismounted. Haskell and two of his men greeted him just inside the doorway of the building.

"Something I can do for you, Fargo?" Haskell asked with his usual expansiveness.

"Just stopping by. Heard you had some trouble with your girls," Fargo said.

"Trouble?" Haskell scoffed. "I wouldn't say that. Just the usual thing. They come here, decide they can hold me up for more money. When I don't give in, they leave. Not all of them, of course."

Fargo turned Haskell's answer in his mind. The man didn't seem at all concerned and his voice had a false

ring to it, he decided. "Seems I'd be a lot more bothered," Fargo said.

Haskell shrugged as he offered another smile. "It
happens regularly. I'm used to it. I'm bringing in a
new lot now. They'll be here in a few days. Everything's under control but I appreciate your concern,"
Haskell said evenly.

Fargo left with a nod, and rode out of town with the
uneasy, undefined feelings still churning inside him.
Haskell's unperturbed calm still bothered him. So did
the fact that what happened was apparently a regular
occurrence. It all added up to a kind of unreal air he
couldn't shake off, especially when added to the other
little things that continued to poke at him. Fargo
added one more as he slowed in front of Emery
Crater's Casino. As with Haskell's place, many of the
second-floor windows were curtained and a sign had
been put up beside the front doors. "CLOSED TILL WEEK-
END," he read aloud. He was still frowning at the sign
when Emery Crater stepped from the building, his
smile fixed in place.

" 'Afternoon, Fargo. What brings you by?" the man
said.

Fargo cast a glance at the curtain windows. "Your
girls quit, too?" he asked.

"That's right, too many of them," Crater said.

"Strange coincidence," Fargo remarked. "Your girls
and Haskell's both."

"Not really," Crater said. "The girls talk to each
other, come up with the same ideas and act together.
Happens all the time."

"You're bringing in new girls, too?" Fargo queried.

"That's right." Crater smiled amiably.

"Guess I'm not used to so much coincidence." Fargo

nodded as he moved the horse forward, going on through town as thoughts pulled at him. The strange air of unreality had grown thicker with the parade of coincidences. He was still frowning as he halted at the sheriff's office. Willie greeted him wearing a gunbelt and pistol.

"Clothes don't make the man," Willie said. "But they sure do fool people."

"That counts," Fargo said.

"I fed Lola," Willie told him as Fargo slid into a chair.

"Had a talk with Haskell and Crater," Fargo said. "I'm bothered by all this coincidence. Seems it's been a regular thing with them."

"It has. Of course, it's all grown bigger since they hired opera singers," Willie said.

Fargo frowned into space for a moment. "It's becoming a long list," he said.

"What is?" Willie asked.

"All the little things that don't fit right. All the questions that don't really have answers. They've got to fit somehow," Fargo said. "And why do I keep thinking I won't like them?"

Willie shrugged. "Because explanations that don't explain nothing bother you."

"Go to the head of the class." Fargo grunted and looked out the window at the day beginning to draw to an end. "I'm going to stay with it. I want answers," he told himself as much as Willie, and pushed to his feet. "See that Lola has water before you lock her up for the night," he said.

"Will do," Willie said as Fargo walked out to the Ovaro, and slowly rode from town in the darkening dusk. He began to order his thoughts into place as he rode. If he went through the list again, he pondered, put things in order, something might leap out at him; a key, a sign, a clue, something to define the undefined. He began with the first on his list, the number of guards watching and standing over the dance girls. Why so many? It was the same at Emery Crater's as at Haskell's place. Why so many? he asked himself again and moved on to his next item, the tenuous balance between the money taken in and the amount paid out.

It didn't appear to add up and made both enterprises seem hardly worthwhile. Yet neither Bartley Haskell nor Emery Crater were the type to run a business without a very hefty payoff. Haskell stayed in his thoughts, and became the next item on the list. The loss of most of his dancing girls would seem upsetting, perhaps shattering. Yet Haskell hadn't seemed bothered at all. Emery Crater had shown the same disinterested attitude. Actions and reactions that didn't add up, either. Last on his list came Andrea and Ulla. Why were they kept entirely apart from the dancing girls? Why were they put in cabins alone? Despite Andrea's haughty approval, it made no sense and neither Haskell nor Crater were the type to indulge anybody. They had taken the steps for their own reasons. But what were they? Fargo questioned.

He was still reviewing his list with the same frustrating results as darkness fell. Everything related, yet nothing connected. Neither key nor sign rose up for him. Surface appearances refused to satisfy. Frustrated, he turned the pinto into the woods that led to Andrea's cabin. There was something he'd decided to explore but the hour wasn't late enough yet and Andrea's presence beckoned. There was nothing like a surrender to the senses to clear away the turmoil of frustration. There was a purity to erotica, despite what the bluenoses said. A small flash of light caught his eye and he followed it to the cabin to hear Andrea just finishing a set of vocal exercises. She opened the door at his knock, clad in a loose-fitting one-piece dress buttoned down the front.

She fastened him with a haughty stare. "Expected you before now," she huffed.

"Better late than never," he offered.

"A phrase I've never agreed with," she snapped, keeping hold of her haughtiness.

"I can go," he said and started to turn away.

Her hands snapped out and caught hold of his shirt. "Don't you dare," she said and her mouth pressed to his at once, wet and warm and demanding. Once again he was aware of how Andrea's imperious eagerness transmitted its own brand of appeal. She could make one feel chosen to give a command performance. In moments, he lay beside her, enjoying her warm, pillowy breasts against his skin, reveling in the encompassing fleshiness of her body, the smoothness of her olive-tinted skin and large, brown-pink nipples. Soon he was exploring every part of her, the luxuriousness of her dense, V-shaped bush and her soft, full-fleshed thighs clasped around him. The little cabin filled with the cries of her pleasure and once again she hit new notes of heightened ecstasy. Finally, she lay gasping, clutched tightly to him, the embers of passion finally depleted.

She slept almost at once, thoroughly satiated. The moon was past the midnight sky when he swung from the bed and she woke. "Where are you going?" Andrea frowned.

"Some things I want to check out if I can," he told her.

"At this hour?"

"Precisely at this hour," he said and finished dressing.

"When will you be back?" she asked, sitting up. He stared at her for a long minute. "What are you thinking?" she said.

"I'm wondering how you can sit there so naked and be so commanding," he said.

"I'm a soprano," she sniffed and lay back. He left convinced the answer was perfectly reasonable.

Outside, he climbed into the saddle and rode through the darkness into town, his plans formed. Not all the dancing girls had left. Perhaps they'd have some explanations, some answers. He'd have a talk with at least one of them. Cold cash had a way of loosening tongues. Halting alongside of the emporium, he was surprised to see there were still a few of the second-floor windows where light slid from behind the curtains. He started for the door and ducked back as two men emerged and climbed into a buckboard. "Great night," the one said. "Next week for sure."

"For sure," the other answered as they drove away. Fargo waited until they were out of sight and, moving quickly, he went to the door of the emporium and eased it open. Inside, the auditorium was dimly lighted, and his eyes glanced immediately to the corridors beyond the stage. He was about to cross to the nearest one when he drew back. Two men stepped into sight at the entrance to the corridor. Fargo's eyes went to the next corridor over and saw two more men there. There were two at the entrance to each of the corridors, he now saw, the very guards who had shepherded the dance girls off the stage when they had finished. They'd seemed entirely overprotective then and they seemed more so now that most of the girls had left. He stayed in the shadows and watched the men at the corridors. They were definitely on guard, and they definitely put an end to his plans to seek out one of the girls and question her.

He slowly, silently slid his way to the front door and slipped outside. But he'd added one more question to his list and he swore inwardly as he returned to the Ovaro. He didn't need any more questions. He needed explanations. He walked the horse through the silent, dark street, halting at the sheriff's office, and took a moment to slip silently inside. He stood quietly, listening, hearing the sound of Lola's steady breathing from inside the cell, and then silently left. A glance at the night sky told him he could get in a few more hours' sleep before morning, and the aching of his muscles begged him to do so. He rode from town, bedded down beneath a stand of red ash, and sank into the softness of his bedroll. But despite his tiredness, sleep refused to cooperate. His visit to Haskell's place had brought only more unresolved questions that added to the gnawing uneasiness inside him.

When sleep finally fought its way to him, it held him in its grip far longer than he'd wanted. He woke to a sun bright and full on the land. He washed, breakfasted on wild raspberries, and returned to town. Willie was at the office when he arrived and Fargo noted the new pride in Willie's bearing. "Everything under control?" Fargo questioned.

"So far. Had an incident last night but you were right," Willie said. "Folks learn respect instead of contempt. By the way, Emery Crater's opera singer stopped by early this morning."

"Ulla Stenson?" Fargo asked.

"She was looking for you, seemed really upset," Willie said.

Fargo frowned back. "Wonder what that's all about?" he murmured. "I'll stop at her place."

"She said she'd be going to Andrea's cabin to look for you," Willie said and Fargo felt a moment of surprise.

"Thanks," he replied and took a moment to look in at Lola, who rose from the cot in the cell the minute she saw him, her shirt hanging open in the front to show the edges of both modest but high, perky breasts. She made no effort to pull the shirt closed.

"You going to let me out of here, dammit?" she flung at him angrily.

"No plans for that," Fargo said evenly. Lola stepped closer to the bars and dropped the anger from her face, giving him a closer view of the edges of her breasts. They were nicely curved, he noted.

"Please, Fargo," Lola said, a soft sultriness in her voice he'd never heard before. "I helped you. You can't forget that. You're not the kind to forget a favor."

"You tried to kill me. I can't forget that, either," he said calmly.

"I made a mistake," Lola said, the soft seductive tone still playing in her voice. "Everybody's entitled to one mistake."

"Depends on the mistake, honey," Fargo said, and turned to leave but not before noticing that the anger still hadn't returned to her face. As he went into the outside office, he called, "See you later" to Willie and hurried out to the Ovaro, putting the horse into a fast canter as he rode to Andrea's place. He heard them both before he reached the cabin.

"Blast you, you can't sing," he heard Andrea scold stiffly.

"At least I'm not a miniature soprano," Ulla shot back.

"You ever call a truce?" Fargo said as he halted and dismounted. Both women rushed from the cabin.

"I've been looking for you," Ulla said.

"Willie told me," Fargo nodded.

She came to him, one hand clasping his arm, her large breasts touching his chest, but the alarm in her blue eyes was quick to surface. "Something happened, something I saw. I don't know what to make of it," she said.

"Tell me," he said.

"I couldn't sleep last night. I wasn't at all tired. I took the wagon and went for a drive. It was late but it was a warm, lovely night. I finally stopped under a huge tree, and I sat there looking at the landscape and the moon. That's when I saw the girl. She was running fast, but three men on horseback caught her. They knocked her down, hit her, and dragged her away. It was awful. I left the wagon under the tree and followed. I wanted to see where they were going. I've always been curious."

"Stupid's a better word," Andrea said.

"I thought maybe I could help her," Ulla tossed back. "It was plain she needed help."

"What happened then?" Fargo asked.

"They took her to a wagon. They had three more there, near a patch of trees. There were other men there, too, and I saw a lot of other girls. I recognized a few of them from their outfits," Ulla said.

Fargo felt the thought leap into his mind as if with a will of its own. "The dance girls who left Emery Crater," he said. "You wouldn't have recognized the ones who left Haskell."

"That's right, only they didn't look like they left on their own. They looked like they were prisoners. Some were tied together. Some walked like they were drugged," Ulla said.

"Probably were, peyote or neroli. What happened then?"

"I got scared. I sneaked back to my wagon and left. I knew I couldn't help that girl," Ulla said.

"The wagons?"

"They were there when I left. It looked like they were staying."

"Let's find out what this is all about," Fargo said, and turned to Andrea. "You never heard any of this. You go to town you stay mum." She nodded and returned to the Ovaro as Ulla climbed into the wagon.

"You coming back soon?" Andrea asked.

"When I can," he answered and swung the pinto alongside Ulla as she drove off in the wagon. When they reached the road, Fargo crossed and rode up the other side as Ulla frowned at him. "We'll stop at your place first, and get rid of the wagon. You've a saddle you can put on that horse?" Fargo queried.

"There's one in the shed," Ulla said and Fargo tossed a glance at her.

"What made you come looking for me at Andrea's?" he asked.

"Thought you might be there," she said with a touch of coyness.

"Why?" he pressed.

"Remember when you met us in town that morning? Something she said then."

"Such as?" Fargo asked evenly.

"You said you'd be visiting us again. I said I'd be waiting. She said she'd be remembering. What'd she mean by that? What would she be remembering?"

Fargo kept his face bland. Ulla Stenson had her own female acuity, and entirely too much of it. "A talk we had one day about living out here in the West," he answered smoothly. "It was an interesting talk." He kept his eyes on the terrain ahead as he felt her studying him.

"No matter," she said. "You weren't at her place just now. I was glad. I'd have been disappointed in you if you had been."

"Why?" he asked casually.

"You're not a man who'd be satisfied with second-rate lovers any more than second-rate singers," Ulla said smugly.

"Definitely not," Fargo said, keeping his smile hidden. Ulla was showing how ego and jealousy get in the way of acuity. He followed as she turned the wagon across the flat terrain dotted with stands of timber, apprehension taking hold of him as he rode.

6

Ulla led the way, sitting on her horse uneasily, he noticed, and as they moved into open land, Fargo beckoned her into a long line of hackberry. "Can you find it from here?" he asked.

"I think so," she said as she peered out from inside the tree cover. They rode for almost another hour when her hand reached out and curled around his forearm, and she nodded to a large blackjack oak standing by itself. "That's the tree I stopped under. Then I went straight on foot," she said.

"We'll stay in here, long as we can," Fargo said, shooting a glance at the sun, now in the midday sky. Another fifteen minutes passed when the stand of red cedar rose up and as they drew closer, Fargo saw the three wagons in a semicircle.

"They're still here," Ulla breathed.

"They're waiting for something," Fargo noted. "I wonder what." He stayed in the hackberry as they drew closer until they were almost mingling in with the cluster of red cedars opposite the three wagons. All were big Conestogas that could each carry a dozen or more people. He saw a number of young women wandering near the wagons, some tending small fires over which coffeepots simmered. He also saw the guards that stood in a loose circle, forming a perimeter to the makeshift encampment.

"Are they being protected or are they prisoners?" Ulla asked, putting voice to his own thoughts.

"Good question. I've got another," Fargo said. "They left Crater, quit. Why are his guards with them?" Fargo's eyes stayed narrowed at the scene. "Then if the girls left, why are they waiting here?" he added. "I'd like those things answered. There'd be only one way for that."

"What?"

"Talk to some of the girls. But that'd mean getting to them, and I'd never make it. I could get in but they'd spot me damn quickly, even after dark."

"I could do it," Ulla said and he frowned at her. "I'd blend in. They'd just see another girl. They don't know them all. I could move around, mingle with the girls, talk to them."

"No," he grunted.

"Why not?" she challenged. "You can't get in without being spotted, and if they move out we'd have to leave the trees to follow. They'd see us at once." He glared at her even as he knew she was absolutely right.

"No. I don't know what's going on and I have a bad feeling about it," Fargo said.

"You won't know anything unless I can talk to the girls. Maybe the guards are just protecting them. Maybe there's a good reason why they're waiting here," Ulla countered.

"And if there's nothing good about it? A bullet could put an end to your career real quick," Fargo said.

"Are you always given to exaggeration?" she huffed.

"I'm given to not being stupid," he snapped.

"You've some other way to find out what's going on?" Ulla tossed back.

"No, dammit," he admitted.

"Then it's settled. I'll go in soon as it's dark. I'll talk to some of the girls. I'll just blend in. It'll be fun," she said and he saw the excitement dancing in her eyes. She was on her own high, caught up in the adventure, the daring and challenge. It was plainly something she responded to inside herself.

"It's no game, dammit. I won't let you," he said.

She turned a haughty stare at him. "You can't stop me. All I have to do is make a noise and we're both caught."

He felt the incredulousness sweep through him as he stared back at her. "You wouldn't," he said.

"Wouldn't I? You'd be surprised what I'd do to get my way. I'm a soprano, after all," she threw back.

"I'm beginning to dislike that word and what it means," he growled.

She leaned closer and he heard her whispered laugh. "It means we're special, in every way. It means we do what we want to do," she said, swinging from the horse and pulling on his hand. "Sit with me. It'll be dark soon." He dismounted, folded himself down beside her, the frown still on his brow. He sat silently as he wrestled with two things, one he had to agree with, the other he had to accept. She was the only realistic chance to get to the girls. But she was also excited enough, and pigheaded enough, to make good on her threat. He didn't know whether to hug her or hate her. Soprano. He muttered the word. They were plainly a world unto themselves.

The day began to fade and Ulla sat in silence beside him. But he could feel her excitement increasing with each minute of the descending dusk. When darkness began to push away the dusk, he saw small cook fires lighted in front of the wagons. They were not going anywhere, plainly waiting for someone or something. The young women began to wander back and forth from the wagons to warm beef strips over the low flames and Fargo watched as the guards moved along a loose circle. The night came to blanket the land and Ulla soon rose. "I can sneak in now," she said.

Hr rose with her. "You can't walk in from here. There's too much open land. You've got to get closer before you can sneak in and start to mingle," Fargo said. "I still don't like it. What if one of the guards recognizes you?"

"No chance of that. These aren't the same men who were on guard inside at the casino. They're not dressed the same. They're rougher. Besides, didn't you say those guards were still back at the casino?" Ulla said.

"That was at Haskell's place," he muttered.

"I'll bet it's the same at Emery Crater's. Most of the girls left at both places, and so I'm sure most of the guards stayed in both places," Ulla said. Fargo had to concede to her reasoning.

"Follow me," he said and stepped to the edge of the hackberry and dropped onto his stomach, flattening himself on the ground. "Start crawling," he murmured. Ulla lay down beside him and began to inch her way with him across the tall buffalo grass. When he reached the cedars, one of the wagons stood only half a dozen yards away. He saw some eight or nine girls moving back and forth between it and the fires. Fargo's eyes locked on the nearest guard, and when the man strolled away, Fargo's hand pressed Ulla's shoulder. "Now," he whispered. "Walk slowly, casually, and don't draw attention to yourself. Slip around to the other side of the wagon before you come out to mingle with the girls."

Ulla rose to her feet as he stayed flattened on the ground. "Where'll you be?" she whispered.

"Right here, waiting, I hope. Make your way back here right after you're finished. Slowly and casually, remember," he told her.

She nodded and, staying flattened on the ground, he watched her saunter toward the wagon and disappear on the other side. His eyes flicked to the guards at the edges of the encampment. They were keeping a casual watch on the young women who talked beside the fires, paying most attention to those girls near the perimeters of the camp, where they could try to slip away into the darkness. As he watched, Fargo grew increasingly certain that the guards weren't there to protect the girls. Their every move and general attitude was that of jailers, not guards, and his eyes swept the area as he searched for Ulla. He finally spotted her at the furthest of the fires, talking to three of the girls, but his lips drew back in a grimace.

She and the other girls all had their heads together, the picture they gave entirely too conspiratorial. "No, dammit," he whispered to himself. "Lean back." But the words he willed at them were not received. Ulla continued to huddle with the other young women and he saw two of the guards now peering across the small fires at them. "Dammit, break it up! Move away!" he shouted silently as he groaned. The two guards had begun to move toward Ulla and the other three girls, but she was too involved in her whispered conversation to notice. His lips pulled back as he watched the two guards near the small knot of young women. Maybe they'd just break up the whispering, he let himself hope. But the hope shattered as, when they reached the huddled figures, the two guards darted. They seized Ulla as the other girls fell back in fright.

Fargo frowned as he wondered why they had zeroed in on her. Holding her by both arms, they pulled her away and dragged her to the nearest wagon. A figure stepped from the wagon at one of the guards' shout. In the flickering firelight, Fargo saw a man with a hooked nose and tight, thin lips. "Look what we've got here," one of the guards said.

The hook-nosed man stepped to Ulla. "Who the hell are you?" he asked.

"You ought to know. You brought me here," Ulla threw back quickly. She could think fast, Fargo noted with grim admiration. The man's answer was a hard slap across the face which made Ulla's cheek redden at once.

"That's for lying to me," the man said.

"I'm not lying," Ulla tried but he grasped her arm harshly, pulling her wrist up to show the underside of it.

"No number," he said. "We stamped a number on everybody we brought." Fargo cursed silently.

"It washed off," Ulla tried again, not giving an inch.

The man slapped her again. "Not so soon it didn't. It takes a week. Now, where'd you come from and what're you doing here?" the man rasped.

"My horse threw me and I saw the fires," Ulla said but Fargo was already scooting himself backward, staying flat, as he again admired Ulla's quick thinking. But they'd not waste time with more questions. They'd come searching to see if she had company. Reaching the hackberry, Fargo rose to his feet as he took cover in the denseness of the trees. Peering out through the foliage, he saw two of the guards dragging Ulla to one side while others began to search beyond the perimeters of the camp. Fargo's eyes followed the searchers as they fanned out. But they were concentrating on the open land and finally, they returned to the wagons where the hook-nosed one waited beside Ulla.

"Nothing. Couldn't see any hoofprints, either," one of the searchers said. "What do we do with her? Leave her for the buzzards?"

Fargo felt the chill sweep through him. The man's question exploded inside him and his thoughts leaped backward. He saw the slow, wheeling flight of the buzzards once again and he saw their curved beaks tearing at flesh. He saw, with sickening clarity, what was left of the bodies of two young women as he had come upon them on his leisurely way to Bearsville. It was a scene still freshly seared into his mind and now it had suddenly taken on new, forbidding dimensions. The man's question echoed through him again with a new and terrible ugliness. How often had other young women been left for the buzzards? Crater and Haskell swam into his thoughts. Their words had been almost identical and they returned to him: "They quit and leave. It happens all the time."

Did the buzzards happen all the time, too? Fargo asked. The guard's words implied as much and Fargo felt anger pushing through the sick feeling that had clawed at his stomach. The hook-nosed man's voice broke into his thoughts. "No, we'll take her back to Crater. Maybe he'll know where she's from. Soon as the others get here, of course," the man said and Fargo watched him follow Ulla as she was put into the wagon. "Tie her up good," the man's voice drifted out from inside the wagon. Fargo's eyes had become cubes of blue ice as one question of his had been answered. They were indeed waiting. For "others." Staying in the trees beside the horses, he peered through the night as the cook fires began to burn out. The guards came out of the wagon, the hook-nosed man staying inside. The guards took up positions around the encampment, forming a loose circle. He guessed only half had taken their posts. The other half were bedded down inside the wagons until it was time to change watch.

Fargo let the night settle down. He wanted to wait to find out who the "others" were when they arrived, but he didn't dare. He had to get Ulla out before it got any harder. As the night grew deeper with only a pale moon lighting the scene, he left the trees once again. Crawling, he made his way to the wagon where they had put Ulla. He'd have to be quiet and merciless, he realized. It was the only way he could get Ulla out and stay alive. Inching forward in the darkness, he climbed to his feet only when he reached the rear of the Conestoga. He paused, listened, then lifted himself to peer into the interior of the wagon. Slowly, his eyes adjusted to the near blackness, the only light from the pale moon that filtered in from the front of the open wagon. He began to make out the young women sleeping on the floor of the wagon, counting nine of them, pressed against one another.

Some stirred as he peered at them, a few whimpered in their sleep and a few others sobbed fitfully. Fargo's eyes moved to the front of the wagon, and found the hook-nosed man asleep, sitting propped up against the front edge of the wagon frame, a rifle across his lap. His eyes shifted again to see Ulla on the floor, her ankles bound and wrists tied behind her. There was no way she could get up without waking her captor. Fargo swore inwardly as he realized there was no way he could cross to the rear of the wagon without waking at least some of the young women. They'd in turn wake the hook-nosed man, who'd snap awake, spraying bullets. Fargo would be right in the path of them, he realized.

He stepped back and started to edge his way around the wagon. When he reached the front, he saw he was in the sight line of the guards if they looked his way. He peered at them, noting they were not watching the wagon for the moment. Colt in hand, he swung one leg over the top of the tailgate of the wagon and lowered himself silently into the Conestoga. The man stirred but didn't wake, and Fargo brought the Colt down across the top of his head. Because of the awkwardness of his angle, it became a glancing blow, but it was enough. The man's hands fell away and Fargo grabbed the rifle before it crashed to the floor. The man sat where he was, unconscious for now.

Silence was the vital key, and one long step brought Fargo to Ulla. He put a hand gently over her mouth, seeing the fright stark in her eyes until she recognized him. Putting a finger to his lips, she nodded as he drew the thin, double-edged Arkansas toothpick from its calf-holster. He cut her ankle bonds first, then her wrist bonds, and helped Ulla up. Putting her behind him, he climbed back out of the Conestoga, helping Ulla down as his eyes flicked to the guards. They were still idly standing in a loose circle, staring mostly out into the open land.

He started to edge from the wagon with Ulla when he heard sounds from inside the wagon, a groan, and then a curse. "Dammit," Fargo bit out as the curse became a shout. His blow hadn't been hard enough. Fargo's eyes went to the guards, seeing them whirl and stare at the wagons. With another curse, the hook-nosed man stuck his head out of the rear of the Conestoga, the rifle in his hands. He saw Fargo and Ulla, and started to climb from the wagon as he brought the rifle up to fire. His shot blew a hole in the corner of the Conestoga's canvas an inch from Fargo's head. Fargo raised the Colt and fired, and the man toppled forward out of the wagon. But the guards were running toward the wagon, Fargo saw, starting to shoot as they did.

"Run!" Fargo hissed and yanked Ulla with him as he darted around the back of the wagon and ran for the trees. The guards spread out as they ran, but it was too dark and they were firing too quickly, their bullets missing wide. When Fargo reached the trees, he stopped and dropped to one knee beside the trunk of a thick cedar. "Go get the horses," he told Ulla and she ran for the stand of hackberry. Fargo, a small target in the dark against the tree, heard the bullets smashing all around him as the guards neared. He recognized two as the ones who'd found Ulla, and as he fired, both went down split seconds apart. He swung the Colt and two more of the onrushing guards went sprawling as they fell. The others slowed, starting to duck away from Fargo's deadly aim, but his next shot caught one more and the man let out a cry as he twisted and fell to the forest floor.

The others were dropping to the ground before firing back and Fargo rose as Ulla crashed through the trees on her horse, pulling the Ovaro with her. Fargo ran and leaped onto the pinto, and Ulla raced beside him as he headed back into the heavy tree cover. Another handful of wild shots zinged by, and soon there were only shouts and the sound of new footsteps racing to the scene. Fargo slowed the Ovaro, mostly for Ulla's sake. She was having trouble hanging on to her horse. They wouldn't give chase, he knew. They had to stay and keep the girls from fleeing. He slowed again when they were well away from the wagons and drew to a halt where the hackberry began to thin out. He turned to Ulla, peering hard at her.

"You all right?" he questioned.

"I'm holding up, if that's what you mean," she answered and he saw the strain on he face.

"Didn't go the way you expected, did it?" he remarked.

"How could I know they'd stamped a mark on each girl?" she returned.

"Unexpected things come with the territory," Fargo said. "What did the girls tell you?"

"I only had time to learn part of it. Crater brings the girls in as dancers. They soon find out he's really brought them in to be prostitutes," Ulla said. "Seems he recruits girls from all over the country."

"To serve his customers," Fargo said.

"That's right," Ulla snapped.

"That answers two questions on my list," Fargo said. "It explains how Crater is making his money. The admission cost doesn't really matter—the money comes from what he makes on the girls. It also explains why you and Andrea are off in cabins by yourselves. He doesn't want you finding out anything about the truth of his operation. You'd likely learn it by girl talk. But that doesn't explain why the girls are being held in the wagons."

"Only some of the girls he brings in agree to do what he wants of them. The rest refuse," Ulla said.

"Those are the ones in the wagons."

"That's right. He ships them out while he brings in a new batch of girls."

"Ships them where?"

"They don't know. He told them he was sending them back where they came from, but they're obviously being held prisoner," Ulla said. "They heard one of the guards say they were waiting for 'the others,' whatever that means. What can we do?"

"Going back now will only get us killed. You can be sure they're all on guard, now," Fargo said. "I'll have to think more on it. Meanwhile, I'm taking you back to your cabin." He moved the pinto forward and Ulla rode beside him, the silence broken only when he asked the question that came to his thoughts along with a host of others. "Was there any mention of Haskell's girls?" he queried.

"No. I'd guess they were kept pretty much apart," Ulla said.

"According to Haskell, most of his girls left, also. I've a real bad feeling about this. I'm thinking they didn't leave by themselves, either. There's too much of a pattern here. Haskell and Crater both bring in high-priced opera singers as star attractions to get in customers. But neither of them make money from admissions," Fargo said.

"We know now how they're making their money," Ulla put in.

"They both bring in girls who quit regularly. It's plain from things I saw that they've been doing it a good while. Both keep the girls in second-floor rooms and well guarded. It's all too much the same. I'm betting that what Crater's doing, Haskell's doing."

"How can we be sure?" Ulla asked.

"Maybe by finding out what they figure to do with the girls they're holding in the wagons," Fargo said. Ulla nodded but fell silent again. The night still veiled the land when they reached the cabin, dismounted, and went inside, where Ulla put the lamp on low.

"What do I do now? Crater will expect me to stop by and rehearse," Ulla said.

"That's exactly what you'll do. Go on as if you don't know a thing. The men who could identify you are dead. They won't be giving any descriptions to Crater. But if you suddenly quit, he might get suspicious. He might arrange an accident for you. Same thing goes for Andrea. I'll fill her in but it's important you both go on as usual. Especially you. You're back in one piece. Let's keep you that way," Fargo said.

Her arms came around his neck. "I'm back because of you. This makes twice." Her mouth came to his, opening at once, her lips soft and pliant. "It's time for two things," she murmured. "To do what I've been wanting to do and to show you a real soprano can sing in lots of ways." Moving backward, she pulled him onto the narrow bed with her and in what seemed seconds, her skirt lay on the floor, her shirt and slip following. As her hands undid buttons on his shirt, he took in her large, deep breasts, as large as Andrea's but very different in shape, thrusting outward firmly, without any apparent softness to them. Very large, deep red nipples were set in the centers of circles that seemed too small for such large breasts. But perhaps the thing he noticed most was Ulla's skin, porcelain white infused with delicate pink, as if she had been dusted all over with powder.

A deep rib cage supported her full, thrusting breasts and a less than flat abdomen offered a fleshy earthiness, as did the dark indentation of her convex belly. Ulla was, he decided, very well covered yet not fat, her flesh tight and firm, all of her larger than she seemed inside her clothes. His eyes traveled downward, and paused, where a surprisingly small, dark triangle sat atop a very prominent pubic mound. Just below, her thighs were full but avoided heaviness, her calves sturdy yet shapely. Her breasts came against him and he felt the firmness and smooth warmth of her pink-dusted skin. She rubbed against him, the feel of her instantly exciting him. She enveloped him, her smooth, warm flesh sending electric messages of the senses.

Her tongue slid forward, tasted and tantalized, in a wet caress and his hand closed around one large, firm breast. "Oh, yes, yes, yes," Ulla urged, a murmur that was somehow a demand. He caressed the pink-white flesh, ran his hand lightly across the deep red nipple, and felt it vibrate as he heard her sharp intake of breath. "Yes, *ja, ja,*" she murmured as her hand came around the back of his neck, pulling his head down between her large breasts, holding him there until he nibbled his way to one red point, caressing the small areola, toying along the edges of the luscious circle. Ulla cried out again, her voice lowering, becoming a throaty moan. Her stomach rose, then fell back as her words became cries.

"More, more, more," she gasped out. Her body followed her words, hard against him, rubbing, urging, the sweet insistence of the flesh. She could surge over one, he saw, over and around and through, giving

Fargo a strangely wonderful feeling of being captured in a net of pleasure. Not responding was out of the question and he felt his own throbbing wanting come over her, pressing down onto the softness of her Venus mound. Ulla screamed and thrust her hips upward at once as her full thighs came open, stretched, and rose to clasp against him. No slow waltz for Ulla, he realized, but an instant bolero of ecstasy, spiraling into increasing heights of pleasure. "Oh, good, oh, good, good, more, more!" she flung out in breathy urgings as she rose and thrust with him, all of her firmness encompassing him, thighs, calves, arms, breasts.

Her cries began to rise as they quickened and he felt himself swept up with her shaking, surging passion, her arms clutching at him, pulling him onto her breasts as her torso rose and fell. She sang out long cries that seemed to dance in the air.

When her arms clasped around his neck, he saw the sudden wide stare come into her eyes, as if she were suddenly in another world. And it turned out she was as her pubic mound all but crashed into him, grinding against him as her full-fleshed body shook. "Now, now, now . . . oh, God, now, now," Ulla demanded and then her voice rose, a towering cry that was a kind of musical scream. He felt himself exploding with her, holding on to her as she shook and drew in tremendous, deep breaths in between screams. He felt her flowing over him, felt all her fleshy contractions that were their own embrace, and knew a new pleasure never exactly known before. But then, that was passion's name, ever the same and ever new, and he'd no quarrel with that.

It was only a matter of minutes, he knew, yet it seemed so much longer, before her thighs fell open and she dropped from his grasp to lie limp on the bed, her breasts rising and falling with each deep breath. Slowly, he saw the glint form inside her sharp, blue eyes, a sly amusement in them as she studied him. "They're so opposite and so the same," she said, musing aloud.

"What's that?" he queried.

"Singing and screwing. One is controlled, the other out of control. But the result is the same, a special kind of pleasure, a special kind of passion," she said.

"And they're both wonderful." He smiled.

"Ummmmm," she murmured, then reached out and pulled him down to her breasts. She sighed contentedly and he was equally content to be half asleep in the aftermath of pleasure, until dawn touched the window. He rose then, and began to pull on clothes.

"Where are you going?" she asked, waking.

"To town, to see Willie and figure if there's anything I can do," Fargo said. She rose up on one elbow, her pink-white skin flushed in the morning light.

"And Andrea?" she asked.

"I'll stop by, fill her in, and tell her she has to go on as usual. It's important you both do," Fargo said.

"I feel sort of sorry for her," Ulla said with a smugness coming into her smile.

"Why?" he questioned.

"She'd like to get you in bed. I know it. But she's too late," Ulla said.

"Too late?" he echoed.

"You've had the best. You're not the kind to be interested in less," she sniffed.

"Good logic," he said as he hurried from the cabin. He rode directly to town to find Willie at the sheriff's office.

"Been worrying and wondering," Willie said at once.

"You had reason to," Fargo said and told him what had happened.

"Still leaves a lot of questions hanging, such as what's going to happen to the gals in those wagons," Willie said.

"And where are Haskell's girls? Are they being taken off somewhere, too?"

"Or is he taking them back where they came from?" Willie wondered.

"I wouldn't put much store in that. He and Crater seem cut out of the same cloth," Fargo said.

"I could snoop around, ask some questions, see who's seen anything or heard anything," Willie offered.

"Good idea. Meanwhile, I'm going back to those wagons," Fargo said.

"That's suicide," Willie said.

"I'll be going alone. I'll stay clear of trouble that way. If the wagons are still there, I'll wait and watch. If they're not, maybe I can pick up a trail that'll give us some more answers," Fargo said. "How's Lola doing?"

"Getting more mean-tempered every day," Willie replied.

"I'll look in on her," Fargo said and stepped into the adjoining room to the cell. Lola came forward at once, unfolding herself with feline grace, her hair washed and neatly brushed, he noticed.

"It's about time you came back," she pushed at him with her lips in a sullen pout.

"Don't take your temper out on Willie. He's not to blame," Fargo said.

"I know who's to blame." She flared.

"Been looking in a mirror?" he said as her lips tightened.

"You're not being fair. You're chasing around with opera singers while I sit here," she accused.

"Who told you I was doing that?" he asked.

"I heard you and Willie talking. They're both after you," Lola said, then softening, she stepped to the bars of the cell, one hand slipping out to rest against his chest. "We could be partners, Fargo. You said so yourself once. They won't stick with you."

"I never make predictions," he said and Lola's softness vanished as suddenly as it had come as her temper flashed.

"Just let me out of here, dammit!" she hissed.

"Haven't had time to think about that," he said and hurried away. Willie waited by the front door. "Just keep feeding her," Fargo told him, then climbed onto the Ovaro and rode from town. He made one more detour and drew up at Andrea's cabin. She came out wearing only her slip, her voluminous breasts hardly contained.

"You took long enough getting back," she said and he heard the suspicion in her voice.

"Had good reason," he said and told her what had happened.

"Guess that is good reason," Andrea said when he finished.

"You shouldn't think the wrong things," Fargo slid at her.

"I wasn't," she returned.

"Hell you weren't." He laughed.

She drew her haughtiness around herself like a shawl. "I wasn't. I knew you wouldn't enjoy her," she sniffed.

"Why not?" he asked.

"You've been with me. You're not going to be interested in an understudy," Andrea said.

"Guess not," Fargo said and marveled at how they not only shared attitudes, but words. "You do your thing for Haskell, as though you know nothing. Sing your arias. Be his star. If Haskell or Crater gets suspicious of either of you, you're both in danger. You could say you're on stage together now, whether you like it or not."

She nodded soberly and came forward, lifting her arms as he slid from the saddle to hold her, marveling at how softness could be the same yet so different. Finally, he disengaged himself from her, returned to the saddle, and hurried away, following the path he'd taken with Ulla to the wagons. It was midday when he reached the thick stand of hackberry, and he rode another quarter mile and dismounted, letting the Ovaro follow as he went carefully on foot. When he reached a place from where he could see the wagons, his lips pulled back in a grimace as he stared out at only empty land. They had gone.

7

He ran from the trees, the Ovaro following obediently behind him, crossing the open land and halting where the wagons had been. His eyes swept the ground at once, the wagon tracks easy to find. The wheel marks showed they had traveled directly south. But they were not alone. His brow furrowed as he saw the wheel marks of at least four other wagons that had joined them. They had all gone south together, accompanied by some fifteen riders. Fargo followed while keeping one eye open for unexpected Shoshone. The landscape grew less tree-covered, drier, with rock formations rising up to take the place of trees. The tracks continued to move straight to the south, deviating only where the terrain forced them to shift direction temporarily.

They passed west of Alamosa toward New Mexico. Brittlebush and paloverde began to show itself though there was still plenty of red cedar and hornbeam stands among the rock formations. He drew to a halt again when he found where they had camped for the night and took note of hairpins, broken combs, and torn bits of blouse left behind when they went on in the morning. The four new wagons stayed with the other three, all moving at a leisurely pace. He reined to a halt once more when he saw the hoofprints of a lone rider leave the others, appearing to be riding back toward Bearsville. Electing to stay on the trail of the wagons, Fargo moved forward when the day wound to a close. He stayed hidden against a rock formation as he rode, finally catching up to the wagons, now drawn together in a half circle.

The Conestogas were all there, but the four new arrivals were Texas wagons with top bows and canvas coverings. He halted, tied the pinto to a straggly young cedar, and climbed onto the ledge of rock. More young women came and went from the four wagons that had joined the others, about forty more, he guessed. The number of guards had also increased, almost doubled, Fargo took note. They made an uneven circle around the wagons as Fargo slid from his rock perch. There were no cook fires, he also saw and it wasn't long before the young women disappeared inside the wagons and the camp fell silent. Fargo let the night deepen and the guards settle into boredom before he moved forward on careful, silent steps.

He made his way to the rear of one of the new wagons, his eyes on the guard standing some dozen feet from it. He decided he couldn't risk trying to crawl into the wagon without silencing the guard. He came up behind the not particularly alert guard, and with one, darting movement, he was at the man, his powerful forearm tightening around the guard's neck. The guard tried to twist free but his breath was already leaving him. Fargo held him still with his other arm. It took but seconds for the guard to lose consciousness, his body going limp as Fargo lowered him to the ground. Swinging himself up over the rear of the Texas wagon, he paused, letting his eyes grow used to the faint light that found its way into the wagon. He counted ten young women asleep, huddled together on the floor of the wagon. He knelt at the head of the nearest one, a slender blonde with long hair.

Her eyes flew open when she felt Fargo's hand over her mouth. "Shhh-hhhh, easy, easy," he whispered. "I'm here to help you." Her eyes peered at him over his hand. "I'm going to take my hand away. Don't scream. Understand?" he asked. She nodded and he removed his hand and pulled her to sit up beside him, her eyes still wide in surprise.

"Who are you?" she whispered.

"Name's Fargo," he said.

"You come to get us out of here?" she asked hopefully.

"Soon as I can find a way," he said. "Wake the girl next to you."

"That's Jenny. I'm Dottie," she said, then bent down to another blond head and gently shook the girl awake. The girl sat up, astonishment in her eyes as she saw Fargo. He nodded at the girl still asleep beside her. "Wake Annie," Dottie said. "Have her wake Elsa. Tell Elsa to wake Carrie." Fargo stayed and waited as one by one the girls were awake and sitting up.

"You're not Crater's girls, are you?" he asked.

"No," Dottie said.

"Haskell's?" Fargo asked and she nodded. He was surprised at only one thing. Apparently, Haskell and Crater found a time to join forces. "Where are they taking you?" he asked.

"We don't know," Dottie said.

"Are you going to get us out of here?" one of the others asked.

"Soon as I figure out a way," he said, managing to

sound a lot more confident than he was. "Tell me everything they've said to you or you overheard."

"Wherever they're taking us, we're all going together, Crater's girls and us," Carrie said.

"They're going to sell us," Elsa said.

"Sell you?" Fargo echoed.

"I heard the guards talking. They're taking us to meet a buyer," one of the other girls said. Fargo felt an icy chill sweep through him and wondered if the girls really realized the meaning of the remark. He decided not to pursue it.

"Somebody left the wagons a while back. I saw the tracks," Fargo said.

"One of the guards. He went to Bearsville. He's going to bring us food. We haven't eaten in three days," Dottie explained.

"They can't use girls who are dead from starvation," Carrie put in bitterly.

Fargo rose. "I'm going now. You never saw me. That's important."

"You coming back for us?" someone asked.

"Somehow, some way," he said and he saw the desperate belief in their eyes. He slipped out of the wagon just as the man on the ground stirred, groaned. Moving at a low crouch, Fargo ran around the other side of the wagon and used the dark of night to return safely to the trees. Once in the saddle, he put the pinto into a fast canter as he retraced the path back to Bearsville. Thoughts swirled through him as he rode. The picture was coming together and it was one of vicious, ruthless depravity on the shoulders of greed. The girls were going to be sold, and the path they were on led toward the Mexican border. That had become clear.

The girls were going to be sold into the white-slave

trade, on one of the principal routes for it reaching across the Mexican border. Once over the border, the girls were doomed. The buyers would take them away in small groups, beyond finding or saving. There, they'd live out the rest of their lives in the lowest class of brothels stretching across Mexico. It was a trade that welcomed getting young women from the north, an infusion of new blood and new dollars, the one following the other. The girls in the wagons knew what lay ahead for them. They just didn't know the hopelessness of their fate. But Fargo felt his own sense of hopelessness tearing at him as he rode. The promises he had made to the girls seemed increasingly hollow.

There were more guards with them now than before. There'd be still more when they were met by the buyers. He had to find a way to get help or he'd have no chance at saving even one of the girls in the wagons. But every plan he ran through his mind ended up the same way—failure. It was still night when he reached Bearsville and he rode through town to Willie Whitten's shack and woke him out of a sound sleep. Splashing water onto his face, Willie chased away sleep as he listened to Fargo with a deepening frown. He crinkled up his face when Fargo finished recounting everything he'd found out.

"They both brought in new crews of dancing girls today," Willie said. "Andrea stopped by, said that Haskell told her she was to sing tomorrow night, they'd be open for business again."

"You can bet Crater's told Ulla the same thing," Fargo said. "Business as usual while their boys handle the sale of helpless girls into slavery."

"From what you've found out, they've been at it a good while. Under the front of being impresarios, they've got a real rotten thing going for them," Willie said. "They're a real pair of vultures."

Fargo nodded as his thoughts went back to that first day when he'd come across the winged vultures on the plains. It had become a significant piece to the puzzle, now. It was perhaps fitting that those vultures should become the key to the acts of human scavengers.

"They sent a rider back to Bearsville to get food," he told Willie.

"Probably from Ernie Hodge. He's the town butcher. He cooks and dries beef strips. He'd be able to supply what they want," Willie said.

"You think we can get a posse up to go after them?" Fargo asked.

Willie didn't hesitate in his answer. "From this town? Forget it. If you had time to do a heap of convincing you'd maybe pick up four or five souls with a conscience. The rest wouldn't lift a finger. This isn't a town with a lot of public-spirited citizens. Haskell and Crater carry a lot of weight. Their operations put money in the hands of too many people, from storekeepers, carpenters, wagoners, dressmakers, and bankers. They're not going to go against something good for their wallets, even if you could get them to believe you."

"Conscience against self-interest," Fargo said gruffly. "Conscience keeps losing."

"You've got me. I'll go with you," Willie offered.

Fargo's smile was wry. "Two of us wouldn't do much better than one," he said, seeing the day come up through the window of the shack. "I'll keep thinking. Maybe I'll come up with something yet, though I'm not holding out a lot of hope." Willie stayed in the doorway as Fargo went outside to the pinto. "I'm going to tell Ulla and Andrea. They should know, for their own protection," he said. "Meanwhile, pay a visit to that butcher. Find out if the food is on its way or if their rider is still here."

"You thinking about stopping the food? Let the girls get hungry enough to revolt?" Willie asked.

"No. That'd only get them killed. Just find out if the food's still here. I haven't decided why yet," Fargo admitted. "I'll stop back at the office."

"I'll be there soon," Willie said and Fargo put the horse into a trot as he rode away. He had decided to stop at Ulla's first, when he met Andrea in her buckboard on the road.

"Follow me," Fargo said curtly, snuffing out her smile. She drove behind him to Ulla's cabin, where Ulla viewed her with a mixture of surprise and displeasure. "We met along the way," Fargo said. "I don't like repeating bad news."

"Is that what it is?" Ulla asked.

"Unless I can come up with more than I have so far," Fargo said, then told them of his visit to the wagons and the bitter answer Willie had given him about a posse.

"This is terrible. You can't just leave them to be sold and taken across the border," Andrea said. "It's barbaric."

"It's the dark side of life in these parts," Fargo said. "I'm sick about it inside but if I go in alone shooting I'll be committing suicide. I'd guess my odds will be about fifty to one."

He waited, saw Andrea frown, glance at Ulla, and bring her eyes back to him. "What if there's no shootout?" Andrea asked. "What if you change their minds

124

about everything?" He saw her and Ulla exchange glances filled with a new excitement.

"What are you talking about?" Fargo asked.

Both of them answered at once. "Simon Boccanegra," they chorused.

"Who?" Fargo asked.

"Simon Boccanegra is the principal character in the new opera by Giuseppe Verdi. It's also the name of the opera. He's the doge of Genoa, one of the independent states in the old Italy," Andrea said.

"He's the what?" Fargo questioned.

"The doge, the head of the state. That's pronounced doe, like in deer, and J . . . Doe—J," Ulla said.

"What's that got to do with a bunch of slave traders?" Fargo queried.

"In the council chamber scene of the opera, the doge faces an angry mob of commoners who want to kill him and take over the government. He's all alone. He can't fight them so he convinces them that what they're doing is brutal and all wrong and in time they'll suffer for it. He convinced them to change their ways. He turned them around, used words as a weapon," Andrea said.

"You could do that with the guards. Face them down. Show them that what they're doing is wrong, selling girls into prostitution for Haskell and Crater. No shoot-out. Logic, conviction, moral pressure," Ulla said. "You're persuasive. You could do it. You need a force to fight them and you don't have it. Turn them around, like the doge did."

Fargo found himself unable not to smile at Ulla and Andrea, the excitement and enthusiasm shining in their faces. "You can't help being sopranos, wanting to just have your way, ignoring anything or anyone else.

You can't help thinking and seeing life as an opera. But then, we're all products of our own worlds. You've just laid out the differences between opera and the real world, between storybooks and life," he said as they frowned back. "The men working for Crater and Haskell don't give a damn about conscience or morals. Money and bullets are the only talk they understand, the only things that'll convince them of anything. If I faced them with a speech about turning good, I'd have so many bullet holes in me I'd look like a sieve."

Andrea and Ulla stared back as dejection slowly replaced excitement in their faces. "That's depressing," Ulla said.

"It's reality," he countered. "But maybe you hit on something. I can't change those bloodsuckers, but maybe I can change the girls."

"Change them how?" Andrea asked.

"From victims to fighters. From kittens to cougars," Fargo said. "I might need your help."

"Whatever you need," Ulla said and Andrea nodded.

"Unhitch your wagons. You'll be riding," Fargo said. "Meet me in Bearsville, at the sheriff's office." Andrea swung from her wagon and Fargo turned the pinto and rode off at a gallop. It was still early morning when he reached town and he drew to a halt as Willie came from the office to meet him. "What did you find out from the butcher?" Fargo asked.

"He sold the rider fifty single bags, a half-dozen beef strips in each," Willie said.

"How long ago?"

"Haskell's man left about fifteen minutes ago with a packhorse carrying the bags in two canvas sacks," Willie said.

"Next question. Can you get me fifty six-guns and extra ammunition?"

"Dave Baker's the town gunsmith. He's the only one who *might* have fifty six-guns in stock," Willie said.

"Go see. Buy them if he has," Fargo said and drew a roll of bills from his saddlebag. "A little left over from the bank sacks. Figured I'd find a good use for it and I have." Willie took the bills and hurried away as Ulla and Andrea rode up. When they dismounted, he took them into the office and paused to look in at Lola. Her eyes swept Ulla and Andrea in one contemptuous glance, then she brought her gaze to Fargo.

"I'm still waiting," she muttered.

"Patience is a virtue," Fargo said.

"Go to hell," Lola flung back as he ushered Ulla and Andrea into the front office. "Don't believe anything he says," Lola's voice followed.

"She's not exactly a fan," Fargo said to Andrea and Ulla as they lowered themselves into two hard-backed chairs.

"I'd say she'd like to be," Andrea murmured. Wisdom and cattiness, Fargo grunted inwardly and marveled at both. "What's happening?" Ulla asked.

"I've come up with a plan. If Willie comes through we'll be in business," Fargo said. "But this means no opera house heroics. It'll mean real bullets, real blood, and you can get real dead. I won't think less of you if you decide to back away. You'd be smart if you did."

Ulla and Andrea exchanged glances, then turned their eyes back to him. "It sounds as though you need us to make it work," Andrea said.

He hesitated, afraid truth would pressure them and he didn't want that. "It might work without you," he said carefully.

"That means it probably won't," Ulla said. He shrugged, refused to add words.

"Count me in," Andrea said. "Sopranos don't back down."

"That's right. They may take time to adjust but they don't back down," Ulla agreed. "I'm in, too."

The sound of Willie arriving outside interrupted Fargo before he could say anything more, but he was afraid they still saw it all in terms of opera, caught up in the romance and excitement of playing a new role. He decided to let it be. They'd made their decision, for good reasons or foolish ones. It wasn't so different from the way most decisions were made. "Got your six-guns," Willie said as he came through the door. "Fifty of them and extra ammo. They're heavy. I brought 'em on a packhorse."

"Let's have a look," Fargo said and the others followed him outside where he saw the two burlap sacks slung over an old mare. He looked into one, pulled out two of the revolvers, one a Smith & Wesson, the other a Remington-Beals pocket revolver.

"There's everything in there, whatever he had," Willie said. "Colts, Remingtons, Starr double-action, Joslyn army pieces, Savage and North, Whitneys, you name it. But they all shoot the same way when you pull the trigger."

"They'll do fine," Fargo said. "We'll put one sack on Ulla's horse, the other on Andrea's." With Willie helping, he transferred the burlap bags and turned to Ulla. "Hit the saddle, ladies. Time's important," he announced and climbed onto the Ovaro.

"We don't know what we're to do," Andrea protested.

"I'll spell it all out when it's time," Fargo replied and

waved back at Willie as he put the pinto into a trot. Ulla and Andrea rode a few paces behind him as he made his way through town, heading southwest. He had gone only a few miles when he halted in country thick with box elder and aspen, and turned to Ulla and Andrea. "I'm going on alone. I'll be riding hard. I have to catch up to that rider with the food. You just keep heading southwest," he directed.

"I thought you were going to spell out things for us," Ulla said. "We can't help if we don't know anything."

"You'll know everything when I get back. You just keep on. Don't push your horses. I'll be back soon as I can," he said and felt their frowns following him as he spurred the Ovaro into a gallop. He let the horse's power eat up the distance as his eyes swept the ground until he found the tracks he sought—two horses, a rider and packhorse, one following exactly behind the other. He swung alongside the tracks as the terrain began to change, picking his way in and out of rock formations and behind long terraces of sandstone. It wasn't long before he spotted the two horses, and he urged the pinto behind a stretch of basalt pinnacles. The rider seemed to be traveling at a leisurely pace. Fargo went past him behind the pinnacles, so he was in position when the rider reached the front edge of the rocky peaks.

Fargo moved the pinto forward to block the rider's way. The man brought his hand to his six-gun at once, resting it there. "Don't even think about it, cousin," Fargo growled. "Get off the horse and you can walk away alive."

"Who the hell are you?" the man questioned, his face tight and weasely.

"Somebody giving you a chance you don't deserve," Fargo said.

"There's no money on the packhorse, just beef strips," the man said.

"Don't want money. Just get off the horse," Fargo said. His gun hand rested lightly against the saddle horn and Fargo saw the man's eyes flick to it as thoughts raced behind his small eyes. He was estimating, calculating, all his conjectures based on experiences facing the ordinary man. "Be smart for a change. Listen to somebody else and dismount," Fargo commanded again. But he saw the man's fingers tighten, his hand start to close around the butt of the gun at his hip. His hand yanked at the gun and Fargo sighed at the predictability of too much ego and too little perception. Fargo's hand moved with a smooth, graceful motion and the lightning speed of a striking rattler.

The Colt fired before the man's gun had barely cleared his holster. With a shuddering motion, the man pitched from his horse and lay still, facedown on the ground. "Stupid," Fargo muttered with more sorrow than anger, then taking the packhorse, he turned back the way he had come. When he spied Ulla and Andrea, he shifted direction and halted before them, swinging to the ground and beginning to tear open the sacks on the packhorse. Ulla and Andrea were at his side as he drew out three of the smaller individual paper bags containing the beef strips. "We put a six-gun into each one of these," he said, and twisted the top of the bag closed. They nodded and began the task as he brought out more of the individual bags. The sun was in the midafternoon sky when they finished putting the revolvers into each bag, and Fargo put one of the burlap sacks onto Ulla's horse, the other on Andrea's. "Let's ride," he said and they started after him.

"It's time we knew the rest of it," Andrea said crisply.

"It is," Fargo agreed as they flanked him. "You'll be delivering the bags, one to each girl, after it gets dark. I could sneak in but I couldn't move from wagon to wagon. They'd spot me too damn quickly. They won't pay any mind to you moving about. The ones who could recognize Ulla are all dead. When we reach the camp you'll go in on your own. You'll tell them Haskell and Crater sent you because he couldn't spare any of his men in town."

"What happened to the man they sent?" Andrea queried.

"He was wounded in a gunfight in town. He couldn't ride but he could give you instructions to get here," Fargo said. They nodded, understanding. "Now, when you're inside the wagons, passing out the food bags, you'll show each girl the gun in her bag. Tell them they're going to set themselves free."

Andrea frowned at him. "They're not sharpshooters, at least most of them won't be. They can't outgun the guards in a fight," she said.

"They can if they do exactly as I lay it out for you. They'll have one big advantage—surprise. They won't have to be sharpshooters. All they have to do is keep shooting." He saw Andrea's face still cling to her skepticism. "Here's how I see it work. I expect the buyers from south of the border will show sometime tomorrow to take their cargo back to Mexico. When they come, the guards will call the girls out of the wagons. But the girls don't move. They don't come out. They stay in the wagons. The guards will go to pull them

131

out. When they do they'll be in plain sight and close. Perfect targets."

"The girls open fire from each wagon," Ulla said.

"Exactly. But it has to be done right or it'll come apart. They have to fire all at once. Anybody fires too soon, the guards will have a chance to take cover and surprise is wasted," Fargo said.

"They'll be in nine wagons. How are they going to know when to shoot all at once?" Andrea asked.

"When they hear my shot, they open fire from every wagon."

"Where will you be?" Ulla asked.

"Watching from one of the rocks up above," Fargo said. "You have everything straight in your minds?" Both nodded. "When the guards are cut down, the buyers will see only one thing—that something's gone very wrong. I expect they'll turn and hightail it the hell out of there and not look back till they reach the border." Ulla and Andrea fell silent as they rode on alongside him, and when Fargo saw the sun begin to slide toward the distant peaks of the San Juan Mountains, he reined to a halt. There wasn't much farther to go, the terrain told him. "You'll be going on alone from here. It ought to be dark when you reach them. You won't see me but I'll be watching," he assured them.

"One thing more," Ulla said. "I didn't have that stamp on my wrist. It gave me away last time."

"You were passing as one of the girls. You're not this time. They won't be looking for a stamp on your wrist, or on Andrea's either," he said, seeing Ulla visibly relax. Suddenly, the excitement in their faces had given way to sober realization, he noted. "Getting second thoughts?" he inquired.

Both lifted their chins at once. "No," Ulla snapped.

"Everyone gets a moment of stagefright before an important performance."

"It's normal. Helpful, sometimes. Gets the blood going," Andrea said.

"Good," Fargo replied. "Remember, I'll be watching." He turned and rode away, putting the Ovaro into a fast canter as he moved into the rock formations. Once inside their twisting passages, he slowed and glimpsed Ulla and Andrea as they rode on. Staying more or less abreast of them but hidden in the rocks, he saw the wagons come into sight as dusk began to blanket the land. Halting behind a basalt ledge, he dismounted, took the big Henry from its saddle case, and moved closer on foot. He finally stopped and crawled up onto the ledge, folding himself behind a low ridge of rock that gave him an unobstructed view of the campsite and enough cover to stay close.

Andrea and Ulla were talking to a half dozen of the guards who had gathered around them. Fargo's finger held steady against the trigger of the rifle. The big Henry's fast repeating action could bring down all six of the men if it became necessary, he knew. His finger remained curled around the trigger until he saw the man step back and Ulla and Andrea lift the burlap sacks from their horses and start to walk toward the wagons. The guards drifted to their positions as night replaced dusk and Fargo felt the knot in his stomach subside. The guards had bought Ulla and Andrea's account. The first, and most difficult, hurdle had been crossed. His eyes went to the wagons, and he saw Ulla and Andrea disappear into the nearest two.

Fargo relaxed and laid the rifle beside him on the basalt rock. Inside the wagons, Andrea and Ulla would be passing out the food bags and explaining the unexpected contents. He imagined them instructing each of the girls on what they'd have to do, emphasizing everything he had stressed to them. He was happy to see how long they stayed in the wagons before Andrea appeared and crossed to the next wagon. It meant they had been thorough in their briefings. Ulla appeared soon after, crossing to another of the wagons. His eyes stayed on the encampment as the moon came up to bestow a tentative, pale light on the scene.

He continued to watch as Andrea and Ulla went from wagon to wagon until they visited the last one together. When they emerged, they crossed to one of the wagons in the center of the half circle and disappeared inside. He smiled. It was the wagon in which they'd chosen to spend the night, the one with the best view of the events that would unfold when tomorrow came. So far, everything had gone perfectly and Fargo settled down for the night behind the rock. The night would be full of nerve-tingling apprehension. So many things could go wrong by the time morning came. The buyers might not show up, or not until the day was almost done. Some of the guards might go into the wagons, then find one of the guns. One was all they'd need to find. Or somebody could drop a gun and it could go off. That'd blow the best-laid plans sky high, Fargo knew.

By morning, every girl in every wagon would be a bundle of tension, their nerves at the breaking point. When the buyers arrived, someone could break and shoot too soon. Surprise, their one advantage, would vanish. Too many things could go wrong, Fargo swore silently. He'd try not to think about them, he told himself, but knew he'd not succeed.

8

Fargo woke with the new sun scorching the land the moment it rose. He had managed to catnap during the night, and now he peered out across the encampment. Some of the guards were using their canteens to freshen up and Fargo saw a few girls leave their wagons, one carrying a small canteen she shared with the others. They didn't go more than a few feet from the wagons and returned almost immediately. At another wagon, he saw one of the girls he had talked to before, Carrie, as she pushed her head out and peered into the distance. She ducked back into the wagon almost instantly and only the guards moved through the camp. Fargo crawled back to the Ovaro and used his own canteen to rub water on his face and neck.

The dryness of nearby New Mexico bathed the camp in arid heat as Fargo watched a gecko scurry across the ground. He turned his eyes south, through the shimmering heat waves as they rose from the ground. Suddenly, objects appeared through the haze, no more than tiny specks. As he peered, the specks grew, taking shape as they drew closer, becoming some fifteen riders and four wagons. Not Conestogas or Texas spring wagons, he noted, but closed converted butcher wagons, and even some closed asylum wagons. Fargo shifted position on the rock, bringing the rifle up in front of him. The new arrivals halted at the edge of the encampment and one dismounted, a squat figure wearing cartridge belts across his chest, a *poblano* atop his head, a large mustache across his upper lip. He talked for a few minutes with Haskell and Crater's men and the guards turned toward the wagons.

"Everybody out," one of them called and Fargo's eyes snapped to the wagons. No one stepped out. "Get out here, dammit!" the guard shouted, louder this time. But again, no one stepped from the wagons. Fargo saw the men exchange angry glances. "God-damn bitches, get out here!" the guard called again. "You want us to drag you out?" The wagons remained still and silent. "That's it. Let's get them damn bitches," one guard said to the others. "Drag 'em out by their hair."

The guards moved forward with an angry murmur, an uneven line approaching the half circle of wagons. They refrained from drawing their guns, Fargo happily noted. For all they knew, all they faced were terrified, helpless girls. Fargo grunted silently, and brought the big Henry to his shoulder. He let them move closer to the wagons, giving the girls targets they'd hardly be able to miss. When the crooked line moved to within a half-dozen yards of the wagons, they started to break into a run. Fargo chose the one in the lead. The rifle resounded against the rocks and the man spun in a circle before he fell. The explosion of gunfire that followed Fargo's shot shook the wagons and sent pieces of canvas flying. Fargo saw almost all the guards go down in the first withering barrage.

A few managed to escape the hail of bullets, and

drew their guns and fired at the wagons as they turned to run. Fargo fired the rifle again and again as both the nearest figures jerked and shuddered as they fell. He spotted a third man at the far edge of the wagons trying to run to where the horses were tethered. The big Henry resounded again and the man dropped in his tracks. Fargo's eyes cut to the Mexican buyers but they were already racing away, wagons bouncing across the cracks in the dry land. As he had surmised, they wanted only to get away from the unexpected ambush, unwilling to be caught by a torrent of hot lead. Above all, they didn't want to be caught north of the border buying girls. He watched them quickly become diminishing spots through the waves of heat and then leaped from the rock and began to trot toward the wagons. Andrea and Ulla were the first out and he was quickly sandwiched between the two of them.

"It worked! It worked!" they squealed and in moments he was surrounded by a crush of young, warm, soft bodies and it seemed everyone wanted to kiss him. There was no reason to resist and finally he stood with two of the girls he had met in their wagon, Carrie and Elsa.

"You did it," Fargo said, taking in all of them.

"No, *you* did it," Carrie and Elsa answered in unison. "We carried it out but you made it happen, your planning, your orders. What can we do for you, Fargo?" Carried continued.

"Take care of yourselves. Decide where you want to go. You've more than enough wagons for all of you to go back to wherever you want," he said.

"Crater hired a lot of us in Nebraska. We'll go back there," one of the girls suggested.

"I'm going home, back to Kansas," another put in.

"You've time, so decide amongst yourselves," Fargo said.

"What about you?" Carrie asked.

"It's not over for me. If I don't get Haskell and Crater, it'll all have been for nothing. They'll just go back to doing the same thing someplace else," Fargo said.

"Can we help? We'll go with you," Elsa offered and the others quickly agreed.

He thought for a long moment. To bring in Haskell and Crater would pose its own set of problems and, as with so many things, numbers didn't always solve problems. "Thanks for wanting to help but I'm saying no," he told them. "You've come through this with nobody wounded or killed. Keep it that way. Go on your ways and good luck. Get on those wagons and get away from here." They nodded solemnly as he turned and motioned to Ulla and Andrea. "Get your horses. Meet me by the rocks," he said and hurried off to retrieve the Ovaro behind the basalt ridges. He was in the saddle when they joined him and they turned east toward Bearsville.

"So Haskell and Crater aren't really rivals," Ulla said.

"They are rivals, but up to a point. They're sure as hell not impresarios interested in spreading culture and providing simple entertainment. Both their operations are a double front—one to bring in girls, the other to bring in customers. You two were strictly window dressing, part of the front for both of them."

"The girls that stayed became part of their whorehouse operation, where Haskell and Crater made their real money," Andrea said.

"That's right, and the girls that wouldn't cooperate

they sold off to south-of-the-border buyers. There's where they stopped being rivals. It made more sense for them to pool their sale of girls—one buyer, one transaction, one payment split between them. I'm guessing they have some secret place they meet for their nonrival business."

"It'll be dark when we get to town. You just going in and arrest them?" Ulla asked.

"It won't be that easy. In fact, it'll be damn tricky. I can't be in two places at once. If I get past their body-guards and arrest one, you can be damn sure some-body will run to tell the other who'll hightail it out of town."

"Why not arrest Haskell and let Willie arrest Crater," Andrea suggested.

"Willie's not ready for that yet. He'll get himself killed and Crater will be gone. But I can't sit back and wait for just the right moment. When their boys don't come back after selling the girls, they'll send some-body to find out why. When they learn what happened they'll both light out for God-knows-where. I've got to find a way to get Haskell and Crater together in one place. It all depends on that," Fargo said.

"Neither of us were there to sing last night. They'll both be furious. We show up tonight they'll want to know why we missed last night. What do we tell them?" Andrea said.

Fargo stared into space as he wrestled with the ques-tion. As he did, an answer rose up inside him, and be-came more than just an answer. "You'll be the spider to the fly," he said as excitement surged through him. Both girls stared at him. "What did the spider say to the fly?" he asked.

"Come into my parlor," Andrea said.

"Exactly, only it won't be your parlor. But the result ought to be the same," Fargo said.

"Make sense out of that," Andrea snapped.

"With pleasure. Listen and you shall learn, both of you," he said. "I'm going to find out if you both can act as well as you sing."

9

Bartley Haskell's anger seemed to fill his small office and his mouth twitched in fury as Andrea stood before him. "Where the hell were you last night, dammit?" he shouted. "I'm paying you to show up and sing."

"I couldn't. I was kidnapped," Andrea said and her voice grew tremulous.

"Kidnapped? You expect me to believe that?" Haskell flung at her.

"They only let me go so I'd come here," Andrea said.

His mouth dropped open. "They? What the hell are you talking about? Who's they?"

"The men who kidnapped me, the ones who are holding the girls in the wagons," Andrea said and saw Haskell's jaw drop open. "They took me there, told me they'd kill me if I didn't do what they wanted. They sent me here with a message for you."

"Message? What message?" Haskell snapped.

"They're through working for peanuts for you and Emery Crater. They said if you want any money from the last sale, you better agree to make them all partners," Andrea said. "They were holding Ulla Stenson, too."

"Crater's singer?"

"That's right. They sent her to give him the same message."

Bartley Haskell's lips drew back in a snarl. "God-damn bastards," he spit out. "What else did they tell you?"

"Didn't need to tell me more. I've eyes. I can see," Andrea said. "They're waiting to hear from you."

Haskell spun and grabbed Andrea's arm, his face red with fury. "You're coming with me," he rasped.

"No," she protested, but found the cold steel of a revolver pushing into her ribs.

"Don't argue with me. Move," he said, gripping her arm as he led her outside, pressing tight against her to conceal the gun. He pushed her through the crowd of customers cheering the dancers, and called out to a man in shirtsleeves as they passed. "Keep 'em dancing long as you can, then close up," he said, and pushed Andrea outside. He gestured to the horse at the hitching post near the door. "Yours?" he asked and she nodded. "Mount up," he ordered and pulled himself onto a bay gelding. "Stay with me. Don't make me shoot you," he threatened. She rode beside him as he hurried from town.

"Where are we going?" she asked.

"None of your business," he snapped.

"I don't understand one thing," she said. "I thought you and Emery Crater were rivals."

"None of your business," he gruffed again. "Now shut up." He spurred the bay into a gallop, left the road, and moved onto a low ridge. Andrea threw quick, surreptitious glances into the trees as she rode beside him. She saw nothing, no fleeting form amid the trees, no quick glimpse of a shadowed rider. It didn't surprise her. Fargo'd be invisible, a wraith in

142

the dark. But he was there. He'd seen her leave with Haskell, she reminded herself, and suddenly felt a chill sweep through her. Haskell had taken her out a side door. He could have missed them. The chill deepened inside her. She was suddenly more afraid than she had been in the wagons waiting for all hell to blow, she realized. Somehow, she hadn't felt so alone, then.

The sight of the house set back in the trees along the ridge interrupted her worried thoughts. A lamp glowed from within one window of the clapboard structure. They halted outside and Andrea saw two horses tethered there, recognizing one as Ulla's.

She dismounted and Haskell pulled her into the house with him. Ulla was in the sparsely furnished room, standing beside Emery Crater, trying not to show the nervousness that was plain in her eyes. Haskell and Crater stared at each other, and Haskell was the one to speak first, his words shooting out like bullets. "It's blackmail, dammit," he said. "We can't let them get away with it."

"No, they'll only keep on doing it," Crater said. He gestured to Ulla and Andrea. "According to them, they want us to come out and deal."

"We'll do it. We'll go along with them, buy ourselves some time. Then the next time we'll be ready for them. We'll wipe them out," Haskell said.

"What about these two?" Crater asked.

"They know too much. We'll have to get rid of them now," Haskell said.

"You're not getting rid of anything," a voice cut in, and Haskell and Crater spun as the tall figure pushed the door open and stepped into the room. "You're over, both of you. You and all the rotten things you've done," Fargo said, his hand resting on the butt of the gun at his side. Both men wore guns under their fancy gray tailored jackets, he was sure, and he hoped they'd draw on him. But both took him by surprise. Moving at the same instantly, they pulled Andrea and Ulla in front of them, Haskell holding Andrea, Crater hiding behind Ulla. Fargo saw their guns pushed into both of the girls' sides.

"Drop your gun," Haskell ordered.

"You sure think alike," Fargo said, not moving.

"The gun—drop it or they're dead," Haskell repeated. Fargo cursed silently. They were too small a target behind Ulla and Andrea.

"You shoot them and you've no more shields. You're both dead. Count on it," Fargo said.

"One last time. Drop the gun," Haskell said and Fargo cursed under his breath. They had the advantage over him. They were callous beyond caring. They'd kill and take their chances. His eyes flicked around the room, pausing on the kerosene lamp against the wall. Thoughts whirled inside him. They'd still have their hostages but not with the same advantage. He'd have mobility, the certainty of bringing them down. They'd know that at once. They didn't care about Ulla and Andrea, only about themselves, and they were men who played the odds.

The Colt leaped into his hands as he twisted away and fired, and the kerosene lamp shattered, exploding into a hundred little leaping tongues of flame as the room was momentarily plunged into darkness. When the lamp shattered, Fargo flung himself in a backward leap, landing in the doorway and rolling outside. He heard the bullets smash into the door and wall as he disappeared outside. Still rolling, he came up on his stomach, the Colt aimed at the doorway. The room was no longer dark as the tongues of flame had leaped onto the old, dry wood as a starving man leaps onto a banquet. Shards of flame instantly began to devour the walls and scurry across the floor, and the acrid smell of smoke was already rising in the air.

Haskell and Crater would come stumbling out with Ulla and Andrea. But their hostages wouldn't be direct shields held in front of them. He'd have a better target for at least a brief moment, and that's all he'd need, Fargo knew. He waited, his finger tight on the trigger. Suddenly, as the fire began to really seize the house, he saw them come out, both men in a crouch, dropping to one knee against the outside wall of the house. Ulla and Andrea were still inside. "Another thirty seconds and nobody will get in there!" Crater shouted. "Thirty seconds. That's all you've got. You can shoot it out with us or go in and get them."

Fargo's eyes went to the windows of the house and saw the leaping flames, no small tongues of fire now but a roaring, consuming fire fed by the old, dry wood. He saw Haskell and Crater rise and start to run toward their horses and he cursed their ruthless cleverness. Pushing to his feet, he raced for the open doorway and skidded to a halt, letting a swirl of flame leap across the room in front of him as he peered through fire and smoke. He found Andrea first, then Ulla. Both had been knocked unconscious and he looked to the walls, now an inferno of roaring flames, the smoke growing heavier as the fire furiously consumed the room.

He dropped to his stomach, grateful that the fire was still leaping upward, the smoke with it, a layer of air still across the floor. Crawling, he made his way around lines of flame that crisscrossed the wooden floorboards. Reaching the unconscious figures and taking one by each arm, he began to drag them back across the floor. The heat seared him as he crawled, dragging his burden with him. He saw a piece of the ceiling come crashing down a half-dozen feet from him. The heat was wrapping itself around him, beginning to rob him of strength as he desperately squinted through the thick choking smoke to find the doorway. It seemed so close yet so far. He rose, lifted Andrea with one arm, Ulla with the other, and staggered toward the doorway, swaying with each step, his breath now deep harried gasps.

A tongue of fire darted at Fargo and he just managed to turn away from it and keep moving. He felt the cool night air soothe his burning face as he reached the doorway, stumbling outside still clutching the two young women. He fell to his knees, drawing deep drafts of air into his ravaged lungs. After a moment's pause, he dragged them away from the house and against a line of bushes. They were still unconscious, but they were safe. Rage rose up inside him, consuming him as the fire consumed the house behind him. He pushed to his feet and climbed onto the Ovaro. The fire illuminated the area now with a hellish yellow light, revealing the tracks of the escaping men's horses. They had raced east and he followed until darkness made reading the hoofprints too difficult and too slow. His eyes went to the low, young trees and the trail they left as they crashed through them, racing desperately, broken and torn branches left dangling on both sides of their path.

In wasn't long before he heard them ahead, and he spurred the pinto on faster. He drew the rifle from its saddle sheath behind him, glimpsing the two riders as they came into sight. He was coming up fast behind them when they heard him, and a shaft of moonlight let him see the astonishment on their faces as they turned in their saddles. He saw Haskell reach for his gun but the big Henry was already against Fargo's shoulder as he fired. Haskell, both arms flying upward, sailed from his horse as though he were performing some acrobatic piece of trick riding. Swinging the rifle to fire again, Fargo saw Crater dive from his horse, hitting the ground and rolling into the brush. Yanking hard on the reins, Fargo brought the pinto to a halt as two bullets whistled past him. Leaping from the saddle, he hit the ground and dropped low as another shot ripped by, this one much closer. He ducked behind the trunk of a red cedar, and saw a line of underbrush move. Crater was running toward his horse, which had stopped a dozen yards away.

Fargo rose and ran forward, following the movement of the brush. He had the rifle raised and aimed as Crater darted out of the bushes to leap onto his horse. He had one foot in the stirrup when the rifle barked. Crater fell backward and the horse bolted, dragging him along until his foot finally fell from the stirrup. Fargo lowered the rifle and slowly made his way back to the Ovaro. Quick death seemed almost inadequate for Crater and Haskell, he reflected as he swung onto the pinto. A lifetime of hell in prison would have been more fitting for all they had done to so many, for so long.

But it was all over now, all except the final clean up of the evil residue they'd left behind. He rode back through the forest, the scent of burned wood and acrid smoke reaching his nostrils before he reached what was left of the house. He saw Andrea and Ulla, now on their feet, their faces smudged with smoke. They ran to him, holding him between them in a sweet vise. "We were about to start back to town. We didn't know what else to do," Andrea said, relief plain in her voice.

"That's as good an idea as any," Fargo said and they took their horses and rode with him in silence. The new day came just as they reached town. Fargo saw Willie Whitten step out from the sheriff's office as they rode up. "It's done with," Fargo said and Willie nodded approvingly.

"Not in an easy way, I'm thinking," he said.

"No, not in an easy way at all." Fargo smiled. A man stepped from inside the office, a face with strong determination and fiery grit.

"Sam Walker, Fargo," Willie introduced.

"You've come to replace Hank," Fargo said after a moment.

"Doesn't look like I'm needed." Sam Walker smiled. "Willie's been filling me in."

"You're needed," Fargo said and took the badge from his shirt, handing it to the man. "You'll also be needing a deputy," he said with a glance at Willie.

"I've already asked Willie to stay on," Sam Walker replied.

Willie gave a pleased little shrug at Fargo's questioning glance. "Didn't want to disappoint you," he said. "Or myself."

"I'm glad, Willie." Fargo smiled.

"We're going back to the cabins to clean up, then I'm getting the first stage out of here," Ulla said.

"Me, too," Andrea said.

"You're in luck. There are two stages due in later today. One's going east, one north to Wyoming," Willie said. "You'll be taking the one east, I'd guess."

"Definitely," Andrea said as Ulla nodded agreement.

"I'll come see you off," Fargo said.

"I'd like that." Andrea smiled, a knowing look lighting her eyes before she turned her horse and rode on.

Ulla stayed a moment longer, her smile also tinged with private thoughts. "You know I'll be there, too," she said and moved her horse on.

"Let's go inside and talk, Sam," Fargo said. "There are a lot of ends for you to wrap up."

"Such as the new girls Crater and Haskell brought in," Willie said. "Thanks to you they won't be meeting the same end the others did."

"Maybe they'd like to try running the emporium and·the casino on their own," Sam Walker suggested. "If they don't, I'll see that they get back to wherever they want to go. What about Lola? She's still in her cell?" Fargo smiled as he thought for a moment. "It's your call. I can always send her on to prison in Boulder."

"I'll talk to her," he said and rose, striding into the cell where Lola glowered at him instantly.

"Almost gave you up," she said.

"Lucky you didn't—I'm feeling kindly," he said. "I'll get you that ten percent of the bank money and you can be on the afternoon stage north."

Her eyes widened, and she was at the bars in one quick leap, her arms reaching through to hold him by the shirt. "I always knew you'd do the right thing, Fargo," she said, all soft sweetness now.

"I'm not so sure I am," he grunted. "You're getting a chance to make a new life for yourself. Don't waste it." She said nothing but her eyes stayed on him as he walked into the outer office.

The next few hours he spent going over things with Sam Walker, visiting the bank and taking the ten percent out of the retrieved monies. It was afternoon when he let Lola out of the cell, and handed her the canvas sack with the money in it. "I'm walking you to the stage," he said and she fell in step beside him. She had put on a fresh shirt that rested lightly on the upward curve of her breasts, the confident sexuality again striking at Fargo. She didn't say anything until they stopped at the stage. It was not a big Concord but a lighter, short-haul rig called a mud wagon.

Out of the corner of his eye, Fargo saw the big Concord waiting along the other side of the street. He saw Andrea ride up to it in the buckboard, her bags behind her. Ulla came soon after with her things in the other wagon. He felt Lola's tug at his wrist. "They're going back East. I told you they weren't for you," she said. "Stay. Come with me, Fargo."

"Sorry," he said. "Besides, I might be going with them. You never know."

Lola's eyes hardened instantly, her softness turning to cattiness. "What's so special about them? You like 'em just because they can hit high notes?" she speared.

"No, because you can only hit low ones," he said evenly.

"Go to hell, Fargo," Lola spat and swung into the stage.

"I'll look for you there." He laughed and hurried away. He went to the big Concord where the driver had already put everyone's bags on the rack. Leading the Ovaro behind him, he halted beside the stage as the driver climbed up on the seat. Andrea's arms went around him, her pillowy breasts pushing into him, her lips softly warm.

"I won't be forgetting you, Fargo," she said. "Come look me up if you get back East."

He nodded as she stepped back, and he immediately found Ulla's arms around him, her lips enveloping, imprinting promises. "I don't need words, do I?" She smiled possessively.

"Definitely not," he said.

"All aboard!" the driver called out and both girls climbed into the stage, looking fondly out the window at him.

"Thanks for everything, Fargo," Andrea said. "Especially the music we made in bed."

He saw Ulla turn to her, the scowl instant on her face. "The music *you* made in bed?" she echoed and her eyes went to Fargo. "I thought we made the music in bed," she said.

Fargo swung onto the Ovaro. "Enjoy the trip back," he said. "Roll that stage," he yelled at the driver.

"Fargo, damn you! Come back here!" he heard them call out in unison. But he was already riding away at a fast canter. There was a time to stay and a time not to. This was definitely a time not to stay. Sopranos were not big on sharing, of that he was certain.

LOOKING FORWARD!
The following is the opening
section from the next novel in the exciting
Trailsman series from Signet:

THE TRAILSMAN #216
HIGH SIERRA HORROR

*California, the High Sierras, 1860—where
an unnatural hunger turned a peaceful
mountain valley into a hell on earth. . . .*

The rapid patter of rushing feet brought the big man in
buckskins up off the log he had been sitting on. His
lake blue eyes narrowed, probing the vegetation, as his
right hand dropped to a Colt nestled on his hip.

Skye Fargo had been enjoying a few final sips of hot
coffee before saddling up and heading out. He was
high in the Sierra Nevada Mountains and planned to
go higher still; his goal was to reach a pass that would
take him over the massive wall of rock and on east. For
days he had been traveling through some of the most
rugged, majestic country on the continent. Every-
where Fargo looked, lofty peaks towered to the clouds.
Scores of deep valleys had been carved by swift rivers.
Countless high granite cliffs had been sculpted by an-
cient glaciers. It had been over a week since he last saw
another living soul.

Now, as Fargo pinpointed the direction of the foot-steps, he set his battered tin cup on the log, palmed his Colt, and cat-footed into the undergrowth, moving as silently as a Modoc. When the patter stopped, so did he. Soon soft sniffling and a pitiable whine drew him to where a slender form was slumped against a low boulder. Bedraggled, shoulder-length sandy hair framed slender, quaking shoulders, and a homespun dress, streaked with grime, bore dozens of rips. Sob-bing, the figure clawed at the boulder as if she were trying to tear into it.

To find a lone white woman in the middle of nowhere was surprising enough. To see her in such a state added to the mystery. Fargo took another step, saying softly so as not to spook her, "Ma'am? What's wrong?"

The woman's reaction wasn't what Fargo antici-pated. Her head shot up. A pretty face splotched by dirt and tears, contorted in abject fear. Then a scream tore from her throat. Like a terrified doe, she whirled and bolted, her dress swirling around shapely calves.

"Wait! I won't hurt you!" Fargo called out, but he was wasting his breath. She cast a look of sheer and utter horror at him and ran even faster.

"Damn." Fargo chased, weaving among the pon-derosa pines, holding his own and keeping her in sight, but unable to narrow the gap. He didn't like leaving his stallion and personal effects untended, yet what choice did he have? The woman obviously needed help, whether she wanted it or not. His guess was that she must be lost, that she had strayed from a party traveling through the region, and she was half out of her mind with fear and anxiety.

Fargo paced himself to outlast her. Years of wilderness living had hardened his sinews, lending them steely stamina. He could jog for miles if need be, and it was unlikely she could do the same.

In the end, though, endurance wasn't the key factor. They had crossed a ridge and were flying down a steep slope when the woman glanced back. In doing so, she failed to see a rock in her path and tripped. Her legs flew out from under her. Screeching, she tumbled in a whirlwind of fabric and flesh, end over end, finally coming to rest in a miserable heap among high weeds. Dazed but determined, she struggled to rise.

Fargo reached her before she could. She recoiled, scrabbling backward like a crab, her green eyes as wide as saucers. "I won't hurt you, lady!" Fargo repeated, and shoved the Colt into its holster as added proof. "Please, calm down." He might as well have asked a tornado to stop spinning.

The woman mewed, heaved onto her knees, and pivoted to run off. Fargo couldn't let her, if for no other reason than the very real danger she posed to herself. Lunging, he grabbed her right arm—and suddenly had a berserk wildcat on his hands. Caterwauling, she attacked, her nails slicing at his eyes, at his neck. He barely fended them off. One dug a furrow across temple, another in his cheek.

"Calm down!" Fargo hollered. But she wouldn't heed. He succeeded in clutching her other wrist but all that did was make her madder. She hissed, she kicked, she tried to bite him, to smash her forehead against his chin.

"Listen to me!" Fast losing his patience, Fargo shook her hard enough to snap her upper and lower teeth together. For a moment she stopped fighting and stood there with tears streaming. "That's better," he said. "Now maybe we can talk."

A howl more bestial than human was her answer. Kicks rained on Fargo's shins. He barely kept her from kneeing him in the groin. Backpedaling, he held her at arm's length, the wild gleam in her eyes telling him his words were useless. But he tried once more anyway. "For the last time, I won't hurt you!"

She attempted to knee him again.

"Suit yourself," Fargo said. Before she could so much as blink, he had let go of her left wrist, cocked his arm, and delivered a solid punch to the chin that crumpled her like soggy paper. She groaned, feebly raised a hand, then collapsed, unconscious. "I'm truly sorry," he said softly.

Sighing, Fargo stooped and lifted her. As he hiked back toward the clearing he studied her features. She wasn't much over twenty. Bags under her eyes and hollow cheeks testified to a lack of rest and nourishment. He wondered how long she had been aimlessly wandering. Her shoes or, rather, what was left of them, gave him a clue. Holes dotted the soles and the bindings were in tatters.

A brisk, welcome breeze stirred the trees. It was summer, nature's time of plenty, and the mountains were in full splendor. Game was abundant. A savvy frontiersman like Fargo had no trouble finding enough to eat and drink. If need be, he could live off the land indefinitely. But many could not. Pilgrims fresh from the East often fell prey to the elements, or starvation. City dwellers used to having all their needs met and couldn't rise to the challenge of providing those needs for themselves. People who didn't know the front end of a deer track from the rear end. Folks who, in Fargo's opinion, had no business venturing into the wilds.

The fire had burned low. Fargo deposited her by the log, then checked how much coffee was left in the pot. There was not a lot but it would suffice. Hunkering, he poured the dregs into a cup and carefully let some trickle between her slightly parted lips. She stirred and sputtered but didn't revive.

Fargo imagined that when she was cleaned up and dressed in her fanciest clothes, she'd be a veritable beauty. Even in unconscious repose she had an air about her. She was the kind who would turn any man's head and be the envy of most every woman. "Who are you?" he quizzed aloud, trying a little more coffee.

Coughing violently, her eyes fluttered open. In her wild flailing she almost knocked the cup from his hand. When she saw him, she cowered against the log in raw fear, mewled like a kitten, and shook from head to toe.

"I'm friendly, lady," Fargo assured her. "What's your name? Where are you from?" Getting her to talk would calm her frayed nerves, he figured, but she went on mewling, her forearms over her face as if to ward off blows.

Fargo tried a different tactic. "You must be hungry." Turning to his saddlebags, he rummaged in one and pulled out the pemmican he kept on hand for times when game wasn't so abundant. "Want some?"

Drool dribbled over her lower lip.

"I'll take it that's a 'yes'?" Fargo bantered. From inside his calf sheath he drew his Arkansas toothpick and sliced off a sizeable piece. "Here." No sooner did he hold it out than she practically tore it from his grasp and began to stuff the whole thing into her mouth. "One bite at a time!" Fargo cautioned, involuntarily reaching for her. A banshee wail changed his mind. She partly rose, her posture that of a cornered animal prepared to take flight if he so much as touched her. "You'll make yourself sick, is all," Fargo explained, sinking onto his knees.

She paid him no mind. Chewing lustily, she finished the first piece and held out her palm for another.

Fargo obliged. The woman huddled down low, her white teeth flashing like a wolf's. It reminded him of the time he'd seen three white captives turned over to the military by Apaches. One had been a woman whose mind had broken under the strain of captivity, and she'd acted just like this one. He sensed she was very close to suffering the same fate, if she hadn't already. "Can you speak?" he asked. "Can you tell me who you are?"

Her teeth stopped chomping.

"I can take you wherever you want," Fargo continued. He was sincere. Never mind that it would delay his arrival in Salt Lake City. And if that happened, he'd lose out on a job that paid several hundred dollars he badly needed.

The woman grunted and resumed chewing.

"Do you have kin nearby? Friends? People somewhere must be worried about you. I bet search parties
are scouring the countryside," Fargo noted. If they
were, she didn't care. She simply stared and chewed.
"My name is Skye Fargo," he introduced himself,
thinking it would prompt her to do the same. But all
she did was go on staring and chewing.

Exasperated, Fargo rose and paced back and forth.
He had to do *something* with her. His best bet, it
seemed, was to take her down to Fort Crook. Located
on the north bank of the Fall River, it was the only military post within hundreds of miles. As forts went,
Crook left a lot to be desired, but it did boast a doctor
and several women, the wives of senior officers. Fargo
had stopped over for a night to attend a poetry recital
the wives had put on.

"I hope you don't object to riding double," Fargo
said as he bent to pick up his saddle blanket.

Her response was to scoot forward and snatch the
pemmican. Growling like a mongrel, she bit off a
chunk large enough to gag a bear.

Fargo let her eat to her heart's content. It bought him
time to saddle the Ovaro, throw on his saddlebags,
and douse the fire. She was still gnawing away like a
beaver on a tree when he walked over and offered his
hand. "Time to go, miss." To be honest, he didn't think
it would work. He was convinced he'd need to slug
her again. But she timidly took hold of his hand and
allowed him to pull her erect.

"Well, now, this is a lot better," Fargo complimented
her.

Her rosy lips quirked upward.

Encouraged, Fargo led her to the stallion. "I'll climb on, then pull you up behind me," he said. The saddle creaked as he settled into it. She was gazing up uncertainly, balanced on the balls of her feet. "Your turn." Fargo bent down.

For some reason she was staring at his throat as if mesmerized. He smiled, being as friendly as he could be, but she sprang back as if he were a mountain lion about to pounce, uttered a low, sobbing groan, and fled.

"Here we go again," Fargo muttered. Straightening, he went after her. But he took his sweet time. Rather than panic her into taking another spill, he was content to hold the stallion to a brisk walk. She couldn't outrun a horse. All he had to do was wait for her to tire herself out.

She bore due east, through dense woodland. Occasionally, shimmering sunbeams dappled her lithe figure, accenting the sweep of her long legs and the contours of her nicely curved thighs. The whole while, she clasped the pemmican to her chest as if it were a treasure she would never part with.

To Fargo's recollection, the woods ended in another quarter of a mile, at a switchback that descended into a pristine valley. Beyond the valley were barrier cliffs, but a game trail north of them wound to snow-capped peaks and the pass that would take him over the Sierra Nevadas.

Already the woman was flagging. Every so often she faltered, shuffling as if drunk, then picked up the pace again.

Fargo doubted she would reach the switchback, and he was proven right when she reeled, cried out, and fell to her knees. He walked the Ovaro up alongside of her and waited patiently while she caught her breath. "There's no need for this nonsense," he said after she stopped wheezing. "All I want to do is see you safe to wherever you'd like to go."

She was trembling like a frightened fawn.

"Why are you making this so hard, lady?" Fargo asked. "If I'd wanted to harm you, don't you think I'd have done so by now?"

She directed a quivering finger upward but she wouldn't look directly at him.

Fargo had no idea what to make of it. "Why are you pointing at me? What did I do? You're being—" He stopped, silenced by the faint crackle of undergrowth and the clatter of a shod hoof on stone. Someone was approaching from the northwest—a white man, probably, since Indians rarely shod their mounts. The crack of a twig to the southwest alerted him to the fact that there were more than one. "Friends of yours?" he asked the woman.

She hadn't heard them. Stiffening, she cocked an ear, then surged upright and broke into a tottering run.

Fargo had had enough of her shenanigans. As sorry as he felt for her, he couldn't let her antics get them both killed. Pricking his spurs against the stallion, he rapidly overtook her, swooped low with his arm hooked, and seized her around the waist. The woman struggled but he swung her up in front of him, belly down, not caring if the saddle horn gouged her. She had brought it on herself. From the sound of things, half a dozen riders were converging. He had to get out of there fast.

"This way, boys! I hear a horse!"

Swearing under his breath, Fargo raced to the north. Common sense dictated he stick to heavy timber. But he had only gone a few hundred feet when he spied riders approaching from that direction, too. With potential enemies to the west and south, he was left with no recourse but to head east to the switchback. From the crest, he was startled to see buildings off in the middle of the valley, and even more stunned to behold three riders trotting *up* the switchback toward him. His only avenue of escape had been cut off.

Fargo swung the Ovaro around just as his pursuers burst from the pines. Immediately they fanned out, encircling him. Some were old, some young. All wore homespun clothes and carried rifles or shotguns. A burly character with a flaming red beard and red curly hair pointed a Sharps at him, thumbing back the hammer.

"Hold it right there, you miserable son of a bitch!"

Six other guns were trained on him. Fargo froze, his hands out from his sides so they could plainly see he was unarmed. "Now hold on, mister. There's been a mistake."

The bearded slab of muscle snorted. "There sure as hell has! And you're the vermin who made it!"

Another man, so young he wasn't yet old enough to shave, suddenly piped up, "We've caught you at last! It all ends today!" He looked at the woman. "Melanie? Are you all right? Did this bastard harm you?"

"I found her—" Fargo began, but they wouldn't let him finish.

"Shut up, scum!" barked a scarecrow in a floppy hat who appeared all too eager to squeeze the twin triggers of his double-barreled shotgun. "So help me, I'll blow you to kingdom come if you so much as look at any of us crosswise!"

The arrival of the three men from the valley proved timely. The rest relaxed a trifle, the man with the shotgun beaming at one of the newcomers and declaring, "We did it, Howard! We caught the culprit in the act! The nightmare is over and we can get on with our lives."

Howard was short and pudgy with wisps of ghostly hair poking from under a battered bowler. His clothes were store-bought, including a suit that had seen a lot of wear, and scuffed shoes. The calmest of the bunch, he scrutinized Fargo intently. "So I see, Callum. But he doesn't look anything like I figured he would. I reckon there's no judging a book by its cover, or a murderer by how sane he appears."

"I'm no murderer," Fargo was quick to counter. "As I've been trying to tell these friends of yours, I—" Again he was interrupted, this time by Callum, who kneed his sorrel in close and whipped the heavy stock of the shotgun in a vicious arc. The stock caught him across the back of his skull, nearly knocking his hat off. Dazzling points of light pinwheeled before his eyes. He swayed and would have fallen but others moved in, pinning his arms. His Colt was plucked loose, his rifle yanked from the saddle scabbard.

"Let's hold us a lynching bee, boys!" Callum whooped. "Right here and now!"

Excited yells greeted the suggestion. A rope was produced. But the racket quieted when Howard gestured and said loud enough to be heard over the hubbub, "Not so fast, fellows! We have to do this right. All legal and proper, with a trial and everything. Then we'll string him up from the highest tree we can find and watch him dance a strangulation jig."

Callum was incensed. "You want us to *wait*? Hell, Howard, one of the people this animal murdered was your own brother! Why in hell can't we do it and get it over with? Why go to all the bother of a trial when we know he's guilty as sin?"

Fargo's vision was clearing. He had an urge to break free while they were distracted but two rifles were still fixed on his midriff.

Howard had everyone's attention. "What if word got out, Callum? That the good people of Meechum's Valley went and hung someone, like a pack of rabid vigilantes? Do you think anyone else will ever want to move here?"

"But after all that's happened," Callum said, "folks are bound to understand."

"Only a fool takes others for granted," Howard retorted. "If you've got your mind set, then at least let's call a meeting and put it to a vote. This is too important a decision for us to make alone. Everyone should have a say."

Callum was not exactly tickled by the notion. "I reckon you're right. We take a vote on everything else, so it's only fair we vote on hanging this son of a bitch before we actually do it."

Fargo couldn't let them haul him off. Keeping a tight rein on his temper, he said, "I keep telling you gents, there's been a mistake. I don't know anything about any murders. I found this woman wandering in the woods, lost and in tears."

"Is that true, Melanie?" Howard asked.

The woman had one hand on the saddle horn, the other gripping the pemmican, and was poised for flight. She nervously stared at the ring of anxious faces, not a trace of recognition in her eyes.

Callum reached out to touch her but she drew back. "What's wrong, girl? Cat got your tongue?"

"After what's she's been through, she's bound to be awful scared and a mite confused," Howard said. "Lift her onto your horse real easy-like, so she can ride double with you on the way back." As an afterthought he added, "Then we'll tie this jasper up so he doesn't get any ideas."

"Here, Melanie, take my hand," Callum said, holding it out. He, along with everyone else, was tremendously shocked when she whimpered and flung herself against Fargo, clinging to him as if she were drowning and he were the only thing keeping her afloat. "What in hell?" Callum blurted.

No one was more dumbfounded than Fargo. Just a few minutes ago she had been resisting him tooth and nail. The best he could figure, she was more scared of her would-be rescuers than she was of him. Maybe the pemmican had something to do with it. His act of kindness had reaped a smidgen of trust. Making the most of the situation, he gently draped an arm across her shoulders and said softly, "There, there. I won't let them harm you."

Their expressions were downright comical. They swapped looks of utter amazement, not believing what they were seeing.

Howard scratched his chin, his forehead puckering. "Something's not right here, boys. If this man did what we think he did, she'd hardly be behaving like she is. Could be he's telling the truth."

Fargo quickly said, "So you'll give back my guns and let me be on my way?"

"Not hardly, stranger," said the burly man with the bushy red beard, a farmer by his appearance. "No one with a lick of common sense lets a fox have a free run of the henhouse. No, I say we give you a trial and sort the facts out."

A few swear words escaped Callum. "It's a waste of time, Isaac, but I'll go along with this lunacy if everyone else votes we should." He sneered at Fargo. "Because I know that when all the jawing is done, you'll hang."

Howard wheeled his bay. "The day is still young. Let's light a shuck. We can send riders to all the homesteads and have the meeting this afternoon."

"Just so everyone is home by dark—" Callum said, then caught himself. "Listen to me, will ya? What a dunderhead! We don't need to worry about the Lurker anymore. We've done caught him."

"The Lurker?" Fargo asked. But all the men were turning their horses, about half remembering to keep their rifles on him.

"The Lurker in the Dark," Howard absently answered. "It's what the folks hereabouts have taken to calling the butcher who has been preying on us. He only strikes at night. And what he does isn't fit to describe in the presence of a lady." Howard regarded him thoughtfully. "Of course, if you *are* the Lurker, you already know all this." Assuming the lead, he held his roan to a trot down the switchback and then spurred it into a gallop as they crossed the valley toward the cluster of buildings. They slowed about one hundred yards out.

"I never expected to find a settlement way up here," Fargo commented. "There wasn't one the last time I came through."

Howard twisted in the saddle. "That had to be years ago, then. It was only three autumns past when our wagon train barely made it over the pass and we decided we'd come far enough."

Fargo gazed at the stark, imposing peaks. It wasn't uncommon for pilgrims bound for the Oregon country or cities along the California coast to weary of the weeks and weeks of tiresome, dangerous travel, and put down roots anywhere that suited them. "You brought wagons over Bitterroot Pass?" Fargo was impressed. It was a feat no one had ever done. Bitterroot was well off the regular route, with so many steep grades and other obstacles that it must have taken them a month of Sundays.

"Took us forever," Howard confirmed, "but luckily we got all those who were still alive over before the cold weather set in. We were almost out of food and had no water, and our animals were skeleton-thin. This valley seemed like paradise. Little did we suspect."

There were approaching seven buildings, the biggest bearing a crudely painted sign that read MEECHUM'S DRY GOODS EMPORIUM. In smaller scribble was the claim BEST SELECTION THIS SIDE OF THE MISSISSIPPI. "This Meechum hombre likes to stretch the truth, I see."

"That would be me," Howard said with a self-conscious grin, then shrugged. "A little advertising never hurts."

"You named the valley after yourself?"

"Oh, goodness no. The people who settled here did, out of gratitude." Howard Meechum paused. "I was the one who organized the wagon train. I signed everyone up, hired a guide, made all the usual preparations. But Paiutes killed our guide and I had to take over. Somehow or other I strayed too far south. Thank God we found the pass or our bones would be all that's left of us."

Fargo might have learned more but just then they drew rein in front of the general store. People started coming out from every building. Shouts were raised, questions thrown. Melanie dug her nails into Fargo's arms and peeked at the crowd over his shoulder. "Don't fret. These are your friends." Grasping her securely, he swung his left leg over the saddle and slowly slid to the ground, her lush body molded to his.

The cries grew shrill and insistent, the general tone summed up by one old-timer who rasped, "Is that him? The Lurker? Why haven't you planted him six feet under yet? If you won't, we will!"

Howard was trying to calm them. Fargo moved Melanie under the store's overhang, putting his back to the wall so no one could catch him unawares. He didn't pay much attention to a wide doorway on his left, which proved to be a mistake. For a second later, out of it hurtled a screaming she-cat with a gleaming new butcher knife hiked on high.

"Die, you fiend! *Die!*"